Bahama Betrayal

A Hutch Holub Adventure

By

Hutch Tyler

Dedication

To my beloved wife.

Our life together remains my most cherished adventure of all.

Acknowledgements

To the Fighting Texas Aggie Corps of Cadets Squadron 8 Class of 1996, "The Outlaws", our adventures served as the inspiration for so much of this book.

"OATS"

Table of Contents

About the Author

Hutch Tyler, a proud native of small-town Texas with ancestral roots tracing back to the days of the Republic of Texas, brings over 30 years of combined experience in the military and construction. Tyler has amassed a wealth of expertise and stories as a builder, a combat medic in an airborne infantry unit, and a construction executive working across the United States and the Caribbean. He holds an undergraduate degree in Construction Science from Texas A&M University and a PhD in Organizational Leadership from Southeastern University.

Inspired by his deep understanding of history and personal experiences, Tyler crafts narratives exploring themes of leadership, sacrifice, legacy, honor, courage, adventure, redemption, and healing. His military background and construction career provide a rich tapestry of experiences that fuel his storytelling.

Hands-on leadership and a visionary approach have marked Tyler's professional journey. His love for history and dedication to his family deeply influence his writing. Through his characters and plots, he weaves in elements of his own life, making each story resonate with authenticity and passion.

Looking ahead, Tyler plans to continue the adventures of Hutch Holub and his team, creating a series that delves into new challenges and deeper character developments. Each book in "The Hutch Holub Adventure Series" will build on the last, ensuring a captivating and evolving narrative. Beyond this series, Tyler is committed to writing more nonfiction articles and books on leadership, aiming to inspire and guide others in their personal and professional lives.

"Far and away the best prize that life offers is the chance to work hard at work worth doing."

— **Theodore "Teddy" Roosevelt**

Chapter 1

"Enjoy the little things in life, for one day you may look back and realize they were the big things."

~Robert Breault

The sun blazed high, casting a shimmering sheen over the Bahamian waters that gently lapped at the shore. I stood knee-deep in the surf, the rhythmic push and pull of the waves grounding me, a welcome contrast to the whirlwind of last night's revelations. Beside me, Goose whooped, flinging himself into an oncoming wave, his laughter blending with the distant cries of seagulls.

"Come on, Hutch! Live a little!" he called, flashing a grin as he splashed water in my direction.

I chuckled, shaking off the weight of responsibility, if only for a moment. "You're asking for it," I warned, retaliating with a splash that sent him sputtering.

"Boys will be boys," Gordo remarked dryly from his lounge spot on the sand, dark sunglasses hiding whatever emotion he had behind his words.

"Damn right," Jack chimed in, his competitive streak surfacing as he pointed towards the makeshift volleyball net we had set up earlier. "We playing or what?"

Payton was already at the net, stretching, his grin cocky and self-assured. "Try to keep up, old man."

The game kicked off with friendly jabs and the satisfying thwack of the ball as it sailed back and forth. Under the relentless sun, we dived and leapt, our camaraderie palpable. It was a rare moment of normalcy, a connection we all craved before we faced the unknown ahead.

But even as we played, I caught Goose sneaking glances at the beachside market where his sister set up her stall. She'd followed us here, seeking a new start after escaping an abusive relationship. His playful exterior masked a fierce protectiveness over her, and this trip, I realized, was as much for her healing as it was for our own relaxation.

Gordo kept checking his phone between serves, his mind back home with his daughter, who was due any day now. The thought of becoming a grandfather for the first time tugged at him, even as he tried to keep his focus on the game.

Payton was all fire and intensity, channeling something more profound than just the spirit of competition. I remembered our conversation the night before—his quiet confession about a recent diagnosis. He hadn't told the others yet, and I could see him funneling every ounce of fear and uncertainty into each spike and dive. He was living each moment as if it were a promise to himself.

Hours slipped by as the sun traced its path across the sky. Eventually, the lure of food and curiosity drew us away from the net and towards the island's heartbeat: the local market.

A riot of colors greeted us—vibrant fabrics fluttering in the breeze, fresh fruits and vegetables piled high in a mosaic of richness. The air was thick with the scent of spices, grilled meats, and seafood, beckoning us deeper into the throng of vendors.

"Try this," Payton offered, handing me a skewer of charred fish. The tangy sweetness of the seasoning hit my tongue, an explosion of flavor that made me nod in approval.

"Delicious," I admitted, watching Goose haggle with a vendor over a carved wooden statue. His fluent Spanish earned him a pleased smile and a better price.

"Check these out," Gordo called from another stall, holding up a pair of intricately beaded bracelets. "Thoughts?"

"Sounds good," I replied, imagining the folks back home who would proudly wear these mementos from our journey. Each item we selected had a tale to tell, a memory that would endure long after the sand from this beach had been shaken from our shoes.

Jack returned to us, holding a worn book about local folklore. "There's a lot of history here," he said quietly, flipping through the pages. "Stories of pirates, hidden treasures, and... huh, sustainable energy."

"Speaking of which," I said, feeling a sense of urgency about our complicated situation. "We should head back soon and strategize our next steps."

"Agreed," Jack said, his expression reflecting his determination.

"Final stop before we leave?" Goose suggested, gesturing towards a stall selling exotic fruits. "We can't leave without trying some of these."

"Lead the way," I said, falling into step beside him. We navigated through the crowd, each lost in his own thoughts but connected by a shared mission.

As the sun began to set, signaling the close of another day, I couldn't shake the feeling that we were on the brink of something significant. An adventure that would challenge us, maybe even shape us. But for now, we walked side by side, united and resolute, prepared to confront whatever challenges tomorrow might bring.

The soft glow of string lights bathed the weathered wood of the beachfront bar, the sound of the waves providing a soothing backdrop to our conversation. My boots rested in the sand, traces of grains clinging to the leather like tiny souvenirs. Looking at them, I couldn't help but smile at the sight of my boots on the beach, recalling the saying that you can take the boy out of Texas but not Texas out of the boy.

"Remember when Gordo rigged the engineering lab's door to play the Aggie War Hymn every time it opened?" Jack laughed heartily, the sound blending into the night air.

"I couldn't step foot in there for a week without saluting," Gordo replied, a hint of a smile breaking through his usual stoic demeanor.

"Or when Hutch tried to rope a calf and ended up on his..." Goose's sentence trailed off as our eyes met, the unspoken punchline hanging between us like a shared joke. I knew Goose always knew how to walk the line between humor and respect.

"Texas A&M was in for a surprise when we arrived," I said, raising my glass. "To brotherhood." The clink of our glasses symbolized the strong bonds we had forged and the shared experiences of triumphs and setbacks.

"Brotherhood," they echoed, their voices blending into a harmonious chorus against the backdrop of the sea.

Stepping away from the group, I found myself drawn to the water's edge. The shadows danced on the surface, hinting at hidden secrets below. The scent of salt mixed with seaweed brought back memories of my childhood, a fragrance that had lingered in my dreams for years.

Growing up with Goose by the Gulf of Mexico, we had endless opportunities to explore. I recalled the weight of a fishing rod in my hands, the excitement of a fish tugging at the line, and the pride in my father's eyes when I caught something.

"Big dreams start small, Hutch," my father used to say, his voice weathered by the coastal winds.

As I reflected on the man I had become, the journeys I had taken, and the scars I had acquired, the ocean before me served as a reflection of not just the moon's glow but also a mirror of our true selves—men shaped by our roots, driven by a thirst for justice and the consequences that came with it.

The sun hung low over the Texas plains, a fiery witness to our adventures. I could still feel the rough ropes in my hands as Goose and I lassoed the calves, sweat beading on our brows, dust swirling beneath our boots. Laughter bubbled between us like a wildfire, wild and unrestrained. The animals kicked and charged, matching our youthful energy.

"Gotcha!" Goose shouted, his grin wide as the horizon. His lasso snared a calf's legs, bringing it to a gentle halt. Always the strategist, he calculated each throw with precision, despite his carefree nature.

"Nice one!" I called out, tipping my hat in respect. Our eyes met, a silent conversation passing between us. There was trust, forged in shared adventures and unwavering optimism.

I remembered the endless expanse of the farm before us, our kingdom, our playground. Every tree held secrets, every creek promised treasure. We raced across those fields until the stars painted the sky, dreaming of distant lands we vowed to conquer together.

"Promise we'll always have this, Hutch?" Goose's voice barely carried over the wind.

"Always," I assured him, a pact sealed beneath the Texas sky.

The memory faded as I stood on the Bahamas beach. The ocean connected both worlds—the rolling waves bridging the gap between the carefree boy and the man I had become.

"Beautiful, isn't it?" Gordo remarked, his gaze mirroring mine.

"More than you know," I replied, gratitude settling in my chest. These men, my brothers, were constants in a life of change. I owed them more than words could express.

"Remember chasing those chickens like fools?" Jack chuckled, tossing a shell into the water.

"We couldn't catch them for the life of us," I said, a smile playing on my lips. Goose's laughter joined in, grounding me in the present.

"Yet here we are," Payton added, "ready for whatever comes next."

We fell into a comfortable silence as the last light of day disappeared below the horizon. The future was uncertain, but we could rely on the foundation of our past. The courage from our days on the farm fueled my resolve, and the camaraderie strengthened my spirit.

"Thanks, guys," I said, the words inadequate but necessary. "For everything."

"Wouldn't be anywhere else, Hutch," Goose replied, his hand on my shoulder, grounding me. Together, we watched the stars emerge, guardians of the night, reminding us of the dreams we pursued and the reality we created with our own hands.

"I never expected to find peace like this," Payton confessed, gazing out over the water. "With all that's happening back home... this is rare."

"Peace is hard-won," I agreed, feeling the weight of the world we had left behind. "General Tecumseh Sherman once said, 'The only legitimate object of war is a more perfect peace,' which is one of my favorite quotes. But we have each other's backs. Always."

"Sometimes, I worry," Payton admitted, his voice tinged with vulnerability. "What if we can't maintain the balance? What if the next challenge throws us off?"

"Then we'll find our balance again," I reassured him, watching as the stars began to appear in the darkening sky. "Just like we always do. Together."

Heads nodded in agreement, silently reaffirming our pact beneath the night sky. The fears and dreams we shared seemed less daunting when we stood together as brothers.

"We'll face whatever comes our way head-on," I declared, my determination unwavering. "Just like we tackled those chickens back on the farm."

Laughter filled the air, a comforting sound that united us. Amidst the ebb and flow of the ocean, we found strength not only in our victories but in our unwavering unity, undcterred by danger or consequences.

With sand still clinging to our skin, we entered the beachside restaurant, its walls adorned with nets and seashells. The murmur of conversation and clinking glasses created a soothing ambiance. We settled at a table under a thatched canopy, the ocean breeze gently rustling through the open-air space.

"Look at all this delicious food," Goose exclaimed, scanning the menu filled with local specialties.

"Try the conch fritters," I suggested, recalling past experiences. "They're like a Bahamian version of hush puppies."

We indulged in a feast, the table groaning under the weight of grilled mahi-mahi, spicy jerk chicken, and tangy lime-coconut shrimp. Each bite celebrated the island's flavors, offering a temporary escape from the demands of life.

"Island cuisine is unbeatable," Gordo remarked, a rare smile breaking through his usual seriousness as he savored the peas n' rice.

"Almost," I countered, savoring the heat of the pepper sauce with the sweet plantains on my plate. "But a good steak and cold Lone Star Beer might give it a run for its money."

Our conversation flowed like the rum punch we raised in toasts—smooth, potent, and filled with laughter. In that moment, nothing else mattered beyond the bond of friendship, good food, and shared experiences.

As the night progressed, we gravitated back to the beach, where a bonfire illuminated the starry sky. Embers danced in the air, mirroring the celestial display above. Jack added a piece of driftwood to the fire, creating vibrant hues of green, blue, and red that painted our faces in the flickering light.

"Remember when Hutch ordered us to streak across campus during finals week?" Payton reminisced, his eyes twinkling mischievously in the firelight.

"Dared is more like it," I interjected, recalling the playful challenge. "And only because you said you'd never run naked in public."

"Technically, it was a cold day in hell," Goose quipped, the shared memory bringing warmth to our hearts.

"College adventures, gig 'em," Gordo reflected. "It feels like a lifetime ago."

"Yet here we are," I said, lifting my bottle. "To enduring friendship."

"Cheers to that," they replied, and our bottles clinked—a simple toast to the depth of our connection.

Stories flowed, each one weaving into the fabric of our shared past. In the flickering light, the world's troubles seemed to fade, overshadowed by our collective strength. Surrounded by comrades, the dangers we had faced felt distant, the violence we had witnessed a mere memory.

We sat around the dying fire, a band of brothers shaped by challenges and bound by shared experiences. I reclined on the cool sand, feeling the solid ground beneath me. Above, the night sky was a tapestry of stars, their brilliance painting a picture of infinity. I pulled my hat down, not to block out the stars, but to focus my thoughts.

"Ever think about how many stars have already burned out by the time we see their light?" I pondered aloud, my words lost in the sound of the nearby waves.

"It makes you want to ensure your light shines bright, doesn't it?" Goose remarked, his voice mirroring my contemplative mood.

We gazed at the fading fire, its warmth a distant memory, our shadows stretching across the sand. Tonight, under the gaze of countless stars, we were five friends united by purpose and strengthened by adversity.

"Let's get some rest," I suggested. "Tomorrow will be a busy day planning and building on the center."

"But first... one more beer," Crazy Train added, met with nods of agreement from all of us.

The bar was now quiet, with only a soft murmur of laughter lingering in the air, reminiscent of the sea's secrets whispered to the shore. Catherine, the beautiful bartender we had all met earlier, moved gracefully behind the counter, a stark contrast to the bottles and glasses around her. Her movements captivated my gaze, and we shared a silent conversation through our eyes.

"It's a quiet night," I observed, breaking the silence between us.

"The best kind," she replied, her voice blending with the clinking of glasses. "It gives you space to think."

"Or overthink," I added, my thoughts drifting aimlessly.

Catherine tilted her head, a strand of hair falling over her eye, which she brushed away with a knowing smile. "Sometimes, the right company can turn overthinking into just... thinking."

"Seems risky," I joked, though a flutter of excitement stirred within me.

"Danger is part of the thrill, isn't it?" she challenged, her words hanging in the air.

"Perhaps it is," I conceded, holding her gaze before looking away. There was a mystery to her, a puzzle waiting to be solved behind her smile.

We both retreated into our own thoughts, me with my drink and Catherine closing up the bar.

"Alright, guys," Gordo's voice broke the silence. "I'm heading out for the night."

"Agreed," I replied, a hint of reluctance in my voice.

I stood up from the barstool, ready to leave Catherine's mystery behind when Payton's urgent voice stopped me in my tracks.

"Hey, Hutch, remember how Kate mentioned hearing about Melanie being involved in investment fraud and on the run?"

"Melanie?" The name hit me like a shock, snapping me out of whatever trance I was in, "Damn, Crazy Train, why bring her up now? In the Bahamas?"

"Sorry to ruin the mood, Cap," Payton continued, "but I overheard some guys talking about her in connection to the energy project we invested in. What if—"

"Yeah, Hutch," Jack added, looking concerned, "I heard some rumors too. They say she's somehow involved in the deal. It must have happened recently since we met with the founders right after Indianola."

The unspoken tension in the air was palpable, as we all contemplated the implications of Melanie's involvement in our plans.

Thoughts of Catherine faded away, replaced by the uncertainty and worry brought on by Melanie's sudden reappearance.

"Forget it...and forget about Melabitch. Let's call it a night," I said, trying to sound composed despite the turmoil inside. "We'll address this news tomorrow."

As I glanced back at Catherine one last time, I couldn't help but wonder.

"Goodnight, Hutch, sweet dreams," Catherine's soft voice called out to me.

"Goodnight," I replied, the word carrying a sense of either promise or impending trouble.

Chapter 2

"As a matter of self-preservation, a man needs good friends or ardent enemies, for the former instruct him and the latter take him to task."

—Diogenes

The sun was setting, casting an orange glow on the streets as I made my way to the office. It had been a productive day, and we had made progress on the project that had kept us in the Caribbean after the fishing tournament. The air was filled with excitement, and I had a feeling that tonight would be special.

"Hey everyone," I greeted my friends as I entered the room. "How about we go to Basil's to celebrate our success and have some fun?"

"Great idea, Hutch!" Goose exclaimed, his eyes shining with enthusiasm. The group agreed, and we quickly made our way to the bar.

As we walked, I noticed Gordo's expression change as he received a text. It was from his old unit, asking for help on a mission to protect civilians. Gordo was torn between his duty to his family and his loyalty to his comrades and protecting the innocent.

At Basil's, the atmosphere was lively, but Payton seemed troubled. He was grappling with whether to share news of his illness with the team. The weight of this secret was evident in his eyes.

Entering the bar, we were greeted by a vibrant scene of music and laughter. We found a table in the corner, enjoying the camaraderie around us while still having our own space.

As we settled in, Jack's humor lightened the mood. I felt a sense of relief as we relaxed and savored the moment.

"Here's to a fantastic evening, everyone," I declared, lifting my glass in a toast. "And to the exciting experiences that lie ahead."

"Salud!" the others chimed in, clinking their glasses together before taking a hearty sip of their drinks.

The bar, bathed in a soft glow, quickly filled with energy as we settled in, the buzz of the crowd enveloping us like a comforting embrace. Laughter and animated conversations filled the space, accompanied by the steady rhythm of a classic rock tune playing in the background. The lively ambiance was infectious, fueling my own anticipation.

"Hey, everyone," I began, raising my glass and capturing their attention. "I'd like to make a toast." My friends leaned in, their eyes fixed on me, anticipation hanging in the air. "To the Dowry of Santa Maria and the positive impact it's allowing us to make.

And to the enduring bonds of friendship. To the adventures we've shared, whether in our carefree college days, on battlefields across the world, or in pursuit of history and treasure beneath the waves."

Their faces lit up with genuine smiles as memories of our shared past flooded the room. "To friendship," they echoed, raising their glasses in unison. The clink of glass against glass reverberated through the air, reaffirming our connection.

"Speaking of college," Goose interjected, a mischievous glint in his eye as he exchanged a knowing glance with me. "How about we order a round of our old favorite drinks for nostalgia's sake? You know, to relive the good old days."

I grinned at my longtime companion, recalling the wild nights when we felt unstoppable, ready to conquer the world together. "You're on, buddy," I agreed, flagging down the waiter to place our order.

As the familiar taste of bourbon touched my lips, I was flooded with nostalgia. The memories of carefree days at the Dixie Chicken and Dry Bean Saloon may be distant, but the strong bond we shared remained unchanged. As we reminisced about our college days, I felt grateful for the enduring friendships that had stood the test of time. Our lives had taken different paths, yet we were still a united team, connected by our shared history. Looking at my closest friends around the table, I knew that we would face any challenges together, like brothers.

The laughter of my friends filled the bar, illuminated by the warm glow of lanterns. We sat around a weathered wooden table, enjoying each other's company after a long day. Glasses clinked as Goose and I took turns sharing stories from our childhood adventures on the farm.

"Do you guys remember when we got that old tractor running?" I asked, a smile playing on my lips.

"Of course," Payton replied, his eyes wide with amusement. "You two tried to use it for everything – even plowing the neighbor's field when they were away!"

Goose chuckled, his mischievous brown eyes shining. "We thought, why not put it to good use if we fixed it up?"

I shook my head at the memory, feeling the warmth of camaraderie between us. Working together on the farm had created an unbreakable bond between Goose and me, a connection that carried us through life's challenges.

Looking around the table, I noticed Gordon, who was carefully examining the menu with a thoughtful expression. When he looked up and saw me, a slight smile appeared on his face.

"Hey, how about we order some food so we don't regret this tomorrow?" Gordon suggested with a touch of dry humor.

"Always the responsible one," Jack joked, raising his glass in a playful salute.

"Indeed, Gordon always has a plan," I agreed, acknowledging his practical nature.

"Great idea! What should we get?" Goose asked eagerly.

"I think a mix of sliders, nachos, and conch fritters would be perfect," Payton suggested, scanning the menu for more options.

"That sounds good to me," I said, already looking forward to the conch fritters. "Thanks for keeping us on track, Gordon."

As the night progressed, our conversation flowed effortlessly, much like the drinks we shared. We seamlessly transitioned between lively banter and heartfelt reminiscing, laughing, toasting to our successes, and cherishing the strong bond of friendship that held us together. Looking around at my friends, their faces illuminated by the warm glow of the bar's lanterns, I felt a profound sense of gratitude for the memories we had created and the enduring connection that carried us through life's adventures.

"Feeling up for a challenge?" Payton interjected, his eyes sparkling with excitement as he motioned towards the dartboard in the corner. "How about a friendly competition?"

"Payton, I've been waiting for this moment," Goose grinned, giving him a friendly pat on the back. "Just remember, you're going up against a former military pilot."

"Bring it on," Payton retorted, his grin widening as he stood up, his competitive spirit shining through.

"Count me in," I agreed, rising from my seat and joining them as we headed towards the dartboard.

The dartboard stood before us, its worn surface a testament to the many games played in this establishment. The scent of victory lingered in the air, igniting my competitive drive. Feeling the festive atmosphere, I patted Payton on the shoulder and raised my voice slightly to be heard over the noise.

"How about we up the ante a bit? The loser buys a round of shots for everyone," I proposed, flashing a grin at my friends who eagerly agreed.

Let's go with something strong," Jack suggested, his eyes shining with excitement. "Maybe Wild Turkey in honor of Payton's jarhead roommate, Steve."

"Sure thing, get ready to be impressed," Payton declared confidently, taking aim before launching his first dart towards the bullseye.

As the game continued, the initial tension among us dissolved into friendly banter and playful teasing. Cheers and groans filled the room as darts hit their mark or missed, our camaraderie evident in our easy laughter and genuine affection for one another.

"Hutch seems to be losing his touch," Goose observed with a smirk as my latest throw missed the bullseye by a wide margin. "Too much time at the desk?"

"Enjoy it while it lasts, Goose," I replied with a grin, shaking my head in amusement. "I'm just a bit out of practice, that's all."

"Maybe you're just afraid of losing," Jack teased, his dry humor cutting through the air. "You don't have a reputation to uphold, do you?"

"Watch your back, Jack," I warned in jest, giving him a playful glare. "I might have to resort to some sneaky tactics if you keep that up."

He raised an eyebrow and smirked, undeterred by my warning. "I'm ready for whatever you've got, cowboy."

"The only John Wayne left in this town," I joked, quoting a Big and Rich song, which earned a chuckle from the group.

As the night progressed, our laughter grew louder, and our throws became less accurate. Despite the mounting evidence, I couldn't help but feel proud of the bond we shared and the memories we had created. These were my brothers-in-arms, and I knew our friendship would remain unbreakable.

"Alright," I admitted as Goose's final dart hit the mark, securing his victory. "You win this round, buddy. But remember, there's always next time."

"Next time for sure," he replied, patting me on the back as I headed to the bar to order our celebratory shots. "I'll be ready for you, Hutch. Count on it."

The music swelled, filling the air with a pulsating rhythm that seemed to flow through me. Looking at my friends, I smiled as they surrendered to the beat, their movements becoming more animated and carefree.

"Come on, Hutch!" Gordon yelled over the music, his serious demeanor giving way to the night's festivities. "Let's show these Islanders how we do it in Texas."

I laughed and joined the dancers, our laughter blending with the music as we moved in sync. The joy was infectious, and for a moment, it felt like we were back in college – carefree and wild, free from the responsibilities of adulthood.

Man, I haven't danced like this in years," Goose admitted breathlessly as he twirled Payton around in a comically exaggerated display of grace.

"Neither have I," I agreed, grinning as I watched Jack execute an impressively fluid moonwalk across the dance floor. "But it feels good, doesn't it?"

17

"Feels great," Goose said, pausing momentarily to wipe the sweat from his brow. "Honestly, I can't remember the last time we all let loose like this."

"Maybe we should make a habit of it," I suggested, only half-joking. "After all, we're not getting any younger."

"Speak for yourself, old man," Payton chimed in, smirking as he sidestepped away from Goose's attempts to recapture him. "I'm still a spring chicken!"

"Spring of 1996 maybe," I replied, rolling my eyes even as I laughed at his antics, "but you just keep telling yourself that."

Despite the lighthearted atmosphere and the pleasure of seeing my friends enjoying themselves, I couldn't shake the instinct to keep a watchful eye on them. Years of military training and life-or-death situations had ingrained in me the responsibility to protect those I cared about, and tonight was no exception.

"Hey, you alright?" Goose asked, sensing my momentary lapse into seriousness. "You're not getting all broody on us, are you?"

"Of course not," I reassured him, forcing a smile onto my face. "Just making sure everyone's having a good time."

"Trust me, Hutch," he said, clapping me on the shoulder. "We're all having a blast. Now come on – let's dance!"

And so, we danced, our spirits soaring as high as the notes that filled the air, embracing the joy of the moment and the unbreakable bond we shared. For tonight, at least, we were free.

The night sky stretched above us, a vast canvas of twinkling stars, as we stumbled out of the bar, our laughter ringing through the quiet streets. Arm in arm, we made our way back to our accommodations, sharing stories and reliving memories that had brought us together in the first place.

"Remember that time Goose fell into the creek?" Payton chuckled, his words slurring slightly. "It's a wonder he didn't break his neck!"

"Hey, I was just trying to impress the ladies!" Goose retorted, feigning indignation. We all knew better, of course – he had simply misjudged the distance between the rocks. But it was moments like these, borne of impulsiveness and folly, that had forged our friendship over the years.

"Let's not forget when Hutch saved my ass from that bar brawl," Jack chimed in, a wry smile playing on his lips. "I owe you one, partner."

"More than one, if memory serves," I replied, a hint of amusement in my voice. "But who's counting?"

As we continued to reminisce, I felt a surge of gratitude for the bond we shared and the memories we had created. Our lives had taken different paths, yet we were united by an unbreakable camaraderie that transcended time and circumstance.

"Guys," I began, my voice filled with emotion, "I want you to know how much I appreciate each and every one of you. No matter what challenges come our way, I know we'll always support each other."

"Absolutely," Goose agreed, his eyes showing unwavering loyalty. "We're a family, Hutch. That will never change."

Our pace slowed as we neared our lodgings, not wanting the night to end. Even as we said goodbye and went to our rooms, I sensed a shift – a turning point in our lives.

Lying in bed, I thought back to the night's festivities, the laughter, and camaraderie. I knew our friendship would endure any obstacles, a guiding light in dark times.

"Cheers to us," I murmured to the darkness, raising an imaginary toast to my friends who were like family. "And to the adventures ahead."

The next morning, my phone buzzed on the nightstand. I grabbed it, heart racing at the sight of the caller ID: Jack.

"Hey, what's going on at this hour? We only went to bed four hours ago," I asked, my voice cracking with sleep as I tried to stifle a yawn.

"Something's not right, Hutch," he replied, his tone serious and urgent. "I just received an email from my contact at the investment firm. There's some kind of issue that the company and the founders can't figure out. But that's not why I'm calling. One of the founders mentioned the name Melanie Lancaster."

My thoughts raced as I tried to make sense of Jack's words. This was the third time I had heard her name in as many days. Two times could be a coincidence, but a third time, especially from a founder, was too much. Melanie, the woman who had once captivated Jack with her charm and beauty, only to betray him without hesitation, was back in our lives, her motives as mysterious as ever.

"Jack, please tell me exactly what was said," I urged, my mind spinning with possibilities.

"Alright, listen closely," he began, his voice steady despite the gravity of the situation. Someone, my guess is Melanie, has been secretly buying shares of the company under different names and accounts for months to gain control of the technology. She now holds a majority stake in the company and is planning something significant that has unsettled Wall Street and the investors."

"Damn it," I muttered quietly, clenching my fists in frustration. "We can't let her succeed, Jack. She'll likely sell off or misuse this valuable technology for her own gain."

"Agreed," he replied, his voice filled with determination. "But we need to proceed cautiously, Hutch. We don't know her full plan, the extent of her influence, or who she has on her side. One wrong move could lead to disaster for the company and our investment."

"Then we'll have to outwit her, won't we?" I said, my determination growing stronger.

"Exactly," Jack agreed, "but keep in mind that she has managed to evade authorities and manipulate funds and power to continue her illegal activities. I'll keep investigating to gather more information. In the meantime, be cautious, Hutch. Melanie is a formidable opponent."

"Understood," I replied, ending the call and reflecting on the seriousness of our situation.

As I gazed at the ceiling, a sense of unease and fear crept over me. Our lives were now entangled with a dangerous enemy, and the risks were higher than ever. This was no longer just about a broken heart and a drained college bank account like it was in our A&M days. Melanie had escalated to financial fraud, insider trading, and even rumored involvement in more serious crimes.

"Melanie Lancaster," I whispered to the empty room, my voice filled with a mix of anger and determination, "not again...not this time."

Chapter 3

"All the great things are simple, and many can be expressed in a single word: freedom, justice, honor, duty, mercy, hope."

--Winston Churchill

The dim lighting of the Bahamian bar cast a warm glow on me and my friends' faces as we gathered around a table, our laughter mingling with the upbeat tunes of a local band.

The clinking of glasses punctuated the air, signaling our shared sense of camaraderie and relief. We had earned these evenings – a brief respite from the high-stakes discussions and works that had occupied our days recently.

"Here's to us," I raised my glass, feeling a smile tugging at the corners of my mouth. "And to a well-earned break."

"Airborne!" my friends chorused in agreement, and we drank deeply, savoring the taste of victory and the sweet burn of rum. "Hutch, where's Jack? He's been MIA most of the day."

"He's handling a few things that popped up," I replied, hoping no one would push the question.

Goose asked, "I wonder what Angela's doing," as he leaned back in his chair, a rare moment of quiet following the question. I knew he was thinking about his sister, who was finally finding her footing after years of turmoil. His playful exterior often hid the depths of his caring nature, and this vacation was as much about her new beginning as it was about our relaxation.

Gordo was on his phone again, scrolling through messages from his daughter. She was due any day now, and the excitement of becoming a grandfather for the first time was a constant undercurrent in his thoughts.

Payton's usual bravado remained slightly subdued tonight. I could see the wheels turning in his mind as he considered how to share the news of his diagnosis with the rest of the team. The fear and uncertainty were there, but so was his determination to live every moment to its fullest.

In that moment, even with Melanie in the back of my mind, it felt like the world beyond the bar had ceased to exist. All that mattered were the people seated around me – my team, my chosen family. We let the music wash over us, reveling in the simple joy of being alive and together.

But as I leaned back in my chair, my phone buzzed in my pocket, jolting me out of my reverie. It was an unfamiliar number, but something about the timing of the call set off alarm bells in my head. I glanced at my friends; their brows furrowed with curiosity as they registered the sudden shift in atmosphere.

"Sorry, guys," I apologized, raising a hand to indicate that I needed to take the call. "I have to take this."

"Go ahead, Jack," I responded, turning away from the group.

Jack proceeded to explain that Melanie had not only taken control from the founders but had also managed to transfer all of the company's liquid assets to a Bahamian bank.

"Got it," I replied curtly, my voice filled with restrained anger. "Let's head down to the bar and discuss this."

"Hutch?" Gordo's voice interrupted my thoughts, his concern evident. "What's happening? You look like you've seen a ghost."

I turned back to the table, meeting the worried looks of my friends. The carefree laughter from earlier had disappeared, replaced by a tense silence. They could sense that something was amiss, and I knew I had to fill them in. We were a tight-knit group, connected by more than just shared history.

23

"Guys," I began, my voice heavy with the gravity of the situation, "we have a major issue."

"That was Jack," I explained, my eyes narrowing in concern. After a brief pause, I continued, "It's Melanie. She's betrayed us all. Jack is on his way to provide more details, but it seems she has stolen everything from the green energy company."

Jack arrived shortly after and shared the limited information he had gathered, causing shock to ripple through my friends. Their expressions shifted from disbelief to outrage, their voices rising with questions and anger.

As the initial shock subsided, a determined resolve settled in – we were committed to bringing Melanie to justice, no matter what it took.

"Jack," Crazy Train spoke firmly, locking eyes with Jack. "We've got your back. We'll handle this together."

I hoped that his words would reassure Jack, reminding him that he had our support in this battle. With my friends standing beside us, I knew we would confront this challenge head-on, united by our sense of duty and determination. The once lively atmosphere of the bar now felt heavy with tension, the joviality replaced by a sense of urgency.

"Jack," Goose Guzman spoke softly, barely audible over the murmurs around us. "What's the situation, man?"

I witnessed Jack's clenched fists, feeling the anger and betrayal surging through me like fire. Without a word, he abruptly left the bar, driven by the urgency of the situation. "Jack, wait!" I called out as he departed. We all hurried after him, the cool night air a stark contrast to the stuffy atmosphere inside, stinging our cheeks as we caught up to Jack, who stood with his head bowed, breathing heavily. Footsteps approached from behind, and I knew my friends were close behind.

"Jack," Payton spoke, his tall form emerging from the darkness with the others in tow. His determined blue eyes reflected the strong bond we shared. "We've been through thick and thin together. Whatever the truth may be, we'll face it together." "Okay," Jack responded, his voice steady despite the turmoil within. "Do you believe we can do this? The FBI hasn't been successful..."

"Justice doesn't wait," I declared, leading my friends out into the warm Bahamian night. Despite the gentle breeze on my face, a sense of urgency and anticipation gripped me. "And we don't have to abide by the FBI's rules," I murmured to myself, aware of the challenges ahead. But one thing was certain: we were united, our determination unwavering, ready to confront any dangers to ensure Melanie Lancaster faced the consequences of her actions.

Chapter 4

"Gold medals are not actually made of gold. They are made of sweat, determination, and a rare alloy known as guts."

--Dan Gable

I guided the team back to a secluded table in the dimly lit corner of the bar. Their faces displayed a mix of concern and resolve, silently acknowledging that something significant was on the horizon. I sensed the weight of their trust in me, the unspoken expectation resting on my shoulders.

"Listen up, I understand we are all still processing the recent news," I started, my voice unwavering. The background noise of the bar faded away, leaving only the sound of our collective breaths. "But remember, we have faced challenges together in the past. Each of you is here because you are the most qualified for this task."

I looked at each of them, making sure to establish eye contact. The soldier within me stood firm, projecting strength and determination. My words were deliberate, resonating with authority.

"Recall our time in SF Selection? The grueling tests and trials that pushed us to our limits? It was not just to break us down—it was to build us up, to make us stronger. You all possess skills that set you apart from the rest. We have endured hardships together, trained to adapt and conquer."

A sense of solidarity began to emerge among us, a bond forged through shared experiences and a deep understanding of each other. I could see it in their eyes—a mutual respect born from overcoming challenges and achieving hard-fought victories.

"We're going to need all the skills we've acquired, every ounce of determination," I say, observing as they straighten up, a sense of resolve settling in. "This mission is different. It's personal."

I focus on each member of the group, their faces shadowed under the dim bar lights. "Melabitch, also known as Melanie Lancaster," I begin, the name landing heavily in the air, "has left a trail of devastation in her wake." My voice carries a deep-seated anger and betrayal.

"Fortunately, despite the loss of the investment, we are still in a good position thanks to what we salvaged from the Santa Maria. Even our future generations should be secure. But that's not the case for many others. Will and Jim started Green Energy with dreams and the life savings of friends who believed in them. This wasn't Wall Street money or funds from a billionaire venture capitalist... it was from friends, from family. Melanie doesn't care whose lives she ruins, but we do. By fate or otherwise she chose this energy company. So, we track her down," I tell the team, each word resonating with determination. "We bring her to justice." My friends' expressions harden; their initial worry now transformed into resolute determination. We are no strangers to danger; we have faced it enough times to anticipate its moves.

"Melanie won't stop until she's forced to," I continue, locking eyes with each of them. Their nods convey silent agreement, unspoken pledges to see this through. In their unwavering gazes, I find a reflection of my own resolve.

"Let's make her understand that there are consequences to her actions," I declare, and with that, our pact is sealed. No dissenting voices, no doubts. Just a united front, ready to confront whatever darkness lies ahead.

I scanned the group, all battle-tested and fiercely loyal. "First things first, we need information," I begin, outlining the plan for our pursuit. "Melanie is elusive, but she leaves traces for those who know where to look."

"Bank records, connections, recent sightings," I continue, mentally mapping out the strategy for tracking down a ghost. "We'll divide and conquer, cover more ground. Goose, you're with me on financials. The rest of you choose a lead and follow it. Remember, she's cunning—always a step ahead."

Their expressions reflect solemn determination as they absorb each instruction. I observe them, each nod a silent agreement, an unspoken commitment. This is not just about following orders; it's about combining our collective skills.

"Communication is crucial," I emphasize, aware of the dangers of silence. "We work as a team. Information flows both ways, understood? We are a unified entity, and that's how we'll close in on her."

"Understood, Hutch," they respond in near unison. Their agreement carries a strong sense of unity, with each member fully committed. This team, bonded by shared experiences and sacrifices, understands the gravity of the situation. They have faith in my leadership, and I have faith in their loyalty. Together, we are a formidable force on the horizon of Melanie's impending threat.

"Okay then," I say, feeling the responsibility of leadership settle comfortably on my shoulders like an old, familiar garment. "Let's get to work. Time is not on our side; every moment wasted gives Melanie an advantage and a chance to do irreparable harm to the company."

They nod, a sense of urgency enveloping us like a heavy cloak. We are once again a cohesive unit, moving forward as one towards an unseen adversary. The Siren's song has ended for us; now it's a pursuit.

As I spoke, my thoughts drifted to Goose and his sister, Angela. Angela had narrowly escaped her troubled past, and as one of Melanie's investors, her future was now at risk due to Melanie's betrayal. Goose had confided in me about Angela's struggles, and how this investment was meant to help her heal from deep emotional wounds. His determination to hold Melanie accountable was not just for our team, but also for Angela.

Gordo's phone buzzed once more, and a fleeting smile crossed his face as he read the latest update on his daughter's ultrasound. He had shared with me his fears of not being there to see his grandchild grow up if anything went wrong on this mission. But I knew that same fear drove him to be meticulous in his planning, ensuring that every detail was accounted for.

Payton's determination shone brightly. He hadn't disclosed his diagnosis to the group yet, but he had confided in me. With the early diagnosis, he knew it would be a while before he faced a life-threatening battle, but today's challenge was about leaving a lasting impact. Our eyes met, and I understood the unspoken commitment—we would face this together.

"Mel is slippery," I remark, tapping on the weathered wooden table that had witnessed countless clandestine meetings. "Just like in her previous insider trading case in the U.S., she will have a plan to evade capture—false leads, silenced witnesses, maybe even scapegoats."

Goose shifts, his expression troubled as he considers the various scenarios. "We need to predict her next moves," he states, his voice unwavering despite the turmoil brewing inside him. "Think ahead like she does; stay ahead of the game."

"Exactly," I respond, feeling the familiar rush of adrenaline starting to build up. "We are familiar with her tactics. She may be clever, but so are we. We possess skills she cannot even imagine."

The team leans in, the shared experience of past missions creating an unspoken bond among us. It's akin to planning a military operation; only this time, our target is as cunning as they come.

"Let's discuss worst-case scenarios," I propose, locking eyes with each team member. "If we hit a dead end, she catches wind of our investigation, and she goes into hiding. What then?"

"We adapt," Jack's gruff voice comes from the back. "As always. Strike where she least expects it."

I acknowledge the wisdom in that straightforward approach. Adaptability has been our saving grace on numerous occasions.

"Remember," I assert, my tone resolute, "this is not just about apprehending a fraudster. We are upholding the principles of justice. For every life she has ruined, every deceit she has spun...it ends with us."

"Absolutely," I hear Crazy Train mutter quietly, and I sense the determination building within them, fueled by the prospect of setting things right.

"Then let's divide and conquer," I command, standing tall. "Stay vigilant and watch each other's backs." We have faced challenges before, and if this is another trial by fire, we will face it together.

As everyone disperses to carry out their assigned tasks, I take a moment to reflect, alone with my thoughts. The mission ahead is clear, stark against the shadows of uncertainty. But I march forward without hesitation, the team following closely behind.

Justice does not wait, especially not for Melanie Lancaster.

"Alright, one final opportunity; if there are any uncertainties or queries, now is the time to voice them or forever remain silent," I announce, my voice a low drawl laden with the impending sense of action. We're gathered in the dimly lit corner of the bar, our makeshift headquarters for the night. The overhead light flickers, casting shadows over the determined faces of my comrades, a spectral dance mirroring the seriousness of our mission.

Understanding that a leader's primary objective is to ensure complete alignment within the team, I inquire, "Any uncertainties, any suggestions—let them be known. We act as a unified front." I make eye contact with each individual, inviting them to challenge or contribute. This is not a dictatorship; we operate on trust, forged in adversity and solidified through challenges.

Goose speaks up first, his voice steady yet tinged with doubt. "What if we encounter innocent bystanders, those caught in the crossfire? I'm certain she has used funds from regular investors. Are we prepared to make those tough decisions?"

The room falls silent as we ponder his words. The ethical dilemma is evident—recovering our funds could jeopardize other investments. Gordo's analytical mind is already assessing the options, but the conflict is visible in his eyes. He has a new life awaiting him back home, and the thought of endangering others weighs heavily on him.

"We remain adaptable. We can't foresee every scenario, but we can ensure we are equipped for any eventuality," I reassure them.

"And what about the aftermath?" Payton interjects, his tone softer. "Melanie isn't just a target; she's someone we all knew. Are we prepared to handle the repercussions of taking her down?"

The question lingers in the air, a stark reminder of the emotional toll this mission will exact. We must reconcile our quest for justice with the personal ties we once shared with Melanie. The distinction between right and wrong is blurred, and we must navigate it with care.

A moment of silence ensues, not burdened by hesitation but rather the calm before the storm, the collective breath before diving into the unknown. Crazy Train shifts, his sharp eyes reflecting the strategic mind at work behind them.

Melanie evaded the FBI because she was aware of their impending arrival, he mentions, breaking the silence. "Let's avoid being as predictable as the FBI or any other bureaucratic agency."

"I agree," I affirm. "We must remain flexible, adapt as needed. Keep her on her toes."

"Anything else?" I inquire, scanning the room. "No judgments here— we're all deeply involved."

They exchange glances, a wordless communication that speaks volumes about the trust we've established.

"Let's not underestimate her," Jack cautions, his warning well-received. "She's been ahead of us so far."

"That's why we skip to step three," I respond, a plan forming as we speak. "We anticipate, we counter, and we close in."

"Absolutely," Goose chimes in, the sentiment echoed in the nods around us.

"This is more than just taking down Melanie—it's about seeking justice for her victims."

The group absorbs the gravity of my words, our shared purpose binding us tightly together. We are a united front, a brotherhood forged through common objectives and mutual respect.

"Let's call it a night," I announce, rising to signal the end of the meeting. "Stay vigilant, stay safe."

"Justice will prevail," I whisper to myself as they exit, their footsteps fading into the background—a rhythm of retribution, a beat of accountability.

I linger, allowing the sounds of the bar to fill the void they leave behind. The clinking of glasses, the hum of conversations—it all blends into the background against the pounding in my chest. The plan is in motion, the course set. Now, we wait for the storm to come.

As I depart, I nod to Catherine, the bartender, a silent farewell, and step out into the enveloping darkness. The night air, heavy with impending action, envelops me like a shroud.

Ahead lies uncertainty, a path fraught with shadows and traps.

Chapter 5

"God doesn't give the hardest battles to His toughest soldiers. He creates the toughest soldiers out of life's hardest battles."

--Unknown

The next morning, as we began making plans and preparations, the sun continued its march above the horizon, casting an ethereal glow across the room as we stood in a tight circle, our expressions resolute. The weight of our decision hung heavy in the air, each of us silently acknowledging the gravity of the task before us.

I looked around at my friends, their faces etched with memories of battles won and lost, bonds forged on the battlefield that had only grown stronger over time. "We've always fought for something greater than ourselves," I said, my voice low but unwavering. "And now we're fighting for justice. For everyone who's ever been hurt by someone like Melanie."

"Damn right," Jack muttered, his jaw clenched as he thought about how Melanie had deceived him. "She'll pay for what she's done, and we'll be the ones to make sure of it."

"Remember when we were stationed together in Afghanistan?" Payton asked, his eyes alight with nostalgia. "We had each other's backs through thick and thin. We made it out of there because we trusted one another."

"Absolutely," Gordon chimed in, his voice laced with conviction. "We've been through hell and back together. There's no one I'd rather have beside me in this fight than you guys."

"Alright then," I declared, feeling a surge of adrenaline course through me. "Let's put our doubts behind us and focus on the mission at hand. We track down Melanie, bring her to justice, and make sure she never hurts anyone again."

"Agreed," they replied in unison, their voices filled with resolve.

As we prepared to embark on our dangerous quest, I could feel the strength of our friendship pulsing between us, a force as powerful and unyielding as the ocean that surrounded the island. We had faced countless challenges before, but this time it was personal. And together, we would see this mission through to its end, no matter the cost.

Just as we were about to head out, Gordo's voice interrupted our preparations. "I've just received an encrypted message from a friend at the FBI. It's not good news... Melanie seems to have something up her sleeve. There's talk of a meeting with dangerous individuals, and Melanie's name keeps coming up."

"Dangerous?" I inquired, feeling the tension rise.

"Top of Interpol's most-wanted list dangerous," Gordo responded grimly. "If we can locate this meeting, we might be able to stay ahead of the game."

The weight of the new information hung heavy in the air. The stakes had been raised, and time was running out. Action was necessary, and it was necessary now.

"Change of plans," I declared, urgency evident in my tone. "We'll split into two teams. One will track down the meeting spot, and the other will continue following the money trail. We can't afford to miss either."

The team nodded, understanding the seriousness of the situation. Our mission had become more complicated and dangerous, but our determination remained unwavering. We were prepared to confront whatever challenges awaited us.

"Goose, reach out to our contacts," I instructed, observing as he quickly dialed on his phone. "See if anyone has information on Melanie's location."

"Already on it, Hutch," he responded calmly, despite the gravity of the situation.

34

Turning to Payton, I assigned him a task. "Crazy Train, gather supplies. We may not have a location yet, but get everything we might need – weapons, technology, first-aid kits, everything."

"Consider it done, boss," Payton said with a grin, excitement gleaming in his eyes as he embraced the challenge.

As we continued our preparations, I noticed Jack standing apart, his fists clenched, his expression a mix of anger and betrayal. Approaching him cautiously, I placed a reassuring hand on his shoulder. "Jack, I know this hits close to home for you. But wc'rc all in this together now. We've got your back."

He gazed at me, his eyes a mix of gratitude and pain. "Thanks, Hutch. I just... after we broke up, I knew she was a bad person, but I never expected her to do something like this. I loved her, you know?"

"I understand," I murmured, giving his shoulder a reassuring squeeze. "But we'll ensure she doesn't harm anyone else."

With a final nod, Jack turned away, preparing himself for the task ahead.

"Quite the way to spend a vacation," Goose remarked.

As we exited into the night, the wooden floors creaking beneath our feet, I couldn't help but feel a twinge of nostalgia for the carefree days that had slipped away like the sands of the Bahamian beach. However, there was no going back – we were committed to this mission, to seeking justice for ourselves and others who had fallen victim to Melanie's deceitful allure.

"Alright, gentlemen," I declared, my voice resolute as we confronted the darkness together. "Let's ensure she faces the consequences."

And so, we embarked on our journey into the unknown, prepared to face whatever challenges awaited us, bound by our unbreakable camaraderie and fueled by our unwavering commitment to the pursuit of justice.

Chapter 6

"One always measures friendships by how they show up in bad weather."

--Winston Churchill

As the sun rose over the Bahamian landscape, I called an old military associate, knowing that our bond was still strong despite the years that had passed since we last spoke. The phone rang twice before a familiar voice answered, "Pauly."

"KA, it's Hutch," I said, getting straight to the point. "I need your help."

Ken Abraham "KA" Pauly, a former Texas A&M buddy who now worked for Homeland Security, was quick to respond, "Long time no talk, brother. What can I do for you?"

"Melanie Lancaster," I said, not mincing words. "I need to find her."

"Melabitch... that's a blast from the past. FTC is after her, right?" KA asked, showing surprise. "Didn't think she'd be on your radar."

"It's a long story I'd love to share over a beer one night but for now let's just leave it at she screwed a lot of people out of a lot of money, the team included but she's like a bad penny, always turning up when least expected," I muttered. "She's caused enough trouble, and I intend to put an end to it. We know she's operating in the Caribbean but that's all."

"Yep," he replied. "The last we heard; she was down in the Bahamas. Some high-end semi-private resort, rubbing elbows with the rich and powerful."

"Thanks, KA. You're a lifesaver," I said, jotting down the resort's information as he provided it.

Hey, that's what brothers are for, right?" He paused for a moment. "Be careful, Hutch. Melanie's not the same girl we knew. She's far more dangerous, and you know how these things can get messy. I'll keep digging and let you know if anything comes up."

"Will do, brother. I appreciate the warning." With that, we exchanged goodbyes, and I hung up the phone.

Melanie at a semi-private resort – it made sense. She always had a knack for finding her way into the most exclusive circles. It also explained how she'd managed to hide from the FBI. But now that I had a lead, it was time to call in a few more favors.

I dialed another number, this time to an old friend who had relocated to the Bahamas after our military days. He went by the name of Tack, and he was a man with connections.

"Hey, Hutch!" Tack greeted me enthusiastically. "It's been a while! I hope you're finally down in my neck of the woods?"

"I am but…Melanie Lancaster," I said, getting straight to the point. "I have reason to believe she's down here, hiding among high society. I need your help to track her down."

"Hell of a way to kill a reunion brother. Melanie? That's a name I haven't heard in years." There was a brief silence before Tack continued, "High society means lots of little people on the payroll so trust will be nonexistent so I'm likely to step on some toes. But you've always had my back. Let me see what I can do."

"Thanks, man. I owe you one."

"Consider it repaid for all those times you saved my hide," Tack chuckled. "I'll make some calls, see what I can dig up. In the meantime, come on down. It's always good to see a friendly face."

"Sounds like a plan," I agreed. "We'll be there this afternoon."

As I hung up the phone, I couldn't help but feel a sense of gratitude for the bonds I'd formed during my time in the military. No matter how much time had passed, these men still had my back, and I knew I could rely on them when the chips were down.

"Alright, Melanie," I muttered to myself, determination setting in. "Your game ends here."

The sun was setting on the horizon, casting a warm golden glow over the makeshift operations center we had set up in Tack's swanky beachfront villa. I leaned against the balcony railing, sipping a glass of bourbon, and surveyed my team: Jack, Goose, and Gordo, all gathered around the table, poring over the information our contacts had provided.

"Alright, let's go through this one more time," I said, joining them at the table. "Jack, give me an update."

"Based on what Tack told us, Melanie's been spotted at various high-end parties around Nassau," Jack reported, his voice steady and focused. "But no one's seen her for a few days now."

"Goose, any luck with those financial records?" I asked, turning to our resident tech wizard.

"Actually, yeah. I managed to find the offshore accounts Melanie used to funnel money from her latest con," Goose replied, a smug grin playing on his lips. "And guess what? There have been some recent transactions, all pointing to a private island near Eleuthera."

"Nice work, Goose," I commended, feeling a surge of hope. "That could be where she's hiding out. What do you think, Tack?"

"That corroborates the whispers I've been able to pick up talking to the friends I have that work as staff in those high-end circles," Tack agreed. "But you can't just storm the place. You guys would stick out like a hooker at a Baptist revival."

"Very funny, Tack ... but I do agree," I said, my mind racing with the possibilities. "We'll need eyes on that island, gather intel before we make our move. Goose, is there any way to access satellite imagery of the area?"

"Trust me, Hutch," Goose responded confidently. "With KA's connections at Homeland and a friend at a private satellite company, I'll have high-resolution images of that island in a few hours. They may not be NSA-level quality, but they'll serve our purpose."

"Great," I said, feeling the pieces of the puzzle coming together. "Once we have that, we can strategize and strike where it hurts. Melanie has gotten away with too much for too long."

As the team sprang into action, I pondered the gravity of our mission. Pursuing sunken treasures was one thing, but taking down Melanie Lancaster was a whole different challenge—a mission driven by personal vendettas and a thirst for justice. Despite the FBI also pursuing her, I knew we were the ones capable of achieving this. We were a team united by loyalty and a determination to right the world's wrongs. As darkness descended, a fierce determination settled within me.

"Justice will prevail," I declared in the growing shadows, my voice resolute. "One way or another."

The drone's buzz filled the air as it hovered above us, guided by Gordo's skilled hands on the remote control. His focus was intense as he maneuvered the device over the island, searching for any trace of Melanie.

"Any luck?" Jack inquired, peering at the screen displaying the drone's live feed.

"Not yet," Gordo replied calmly, despite the tension. "I have to fly at the edge of facial recognition distance to avoid detection."

"Keep at it," I urged, my heart racing with anticipation. "We need confirmation before we make a move."

"Understood," Gordo acknowledged, adjusting the drone's position for a better view.

Meanwhile, Jack laid out a map of the island on the table, already planning our approach with precision, considering potential threats and obstacles.

"Assuming Melanie is in one of the private villas," Jack began, pointing to a location on the map, "we should approach from the north. It offers fewer obstacles and keeps most of the resort patrons behind us and to the east."

"Agreed," I concurred, mentally preparing for the operation ahead. "But we need more intel. Melanie won't go down without a fight, so we must be prepared for whatever comes our way."

"Which is why we really need more local information," Jack insisted, his eyes narrowing as he scanned the map for potential weak points. "She's been on the run for months and likely knows this island like the back of her hand. If we can catch her off guard, we'll have a better chance of capturing her before anyone realizes. But that will require more information than we can gather from photos or even NSA-type thermals."

"Agreed," I said, considering our options.

"Well, I think I'm seeing the first evidence of the need for local intelligence," Gordo interjected, his voice tense as he directed our attention back to the drone feed.

On the screen, we could see a group of men milling about near the cove behind the villas. Their movements seemed too purposeful and repetitive for tourists.

"Looks like Melanie's got her own welcoming committee," I muttered, my gut tightening with anger and determination. "We'll need to neutralize them before we can reach her. Otherwise, it will escalate into chaos."

Chapter 7

"Life is partly what we make it, and partly what it is made by the friends we choose."

— Tennessee Williams

The salty sea air lingered in our nostrils as we pushed open the door to the crowded bar. I could feel the bass of the music reverberating through my chest as laughter and conversation filled the dimly-lit room. My eyes scanned the bustling scene, searching for any sign of Catherine.

"See her yet, Hutch?" Goose's voice barely carried over the noise, his dark eyes scanning the crowd alongside mine.

"I wish," I muttered, frustration edging into my tone. We needed to find her quickly. Melanie's trail wouldn't stay warm forever, and if we had any chance of bringing her to justice, we couldn't afford delays.

I took a step forward, my boots grinding against the sticky floor as the smell of stale beer and sweat assaulted my senses. Then I saw her – Catherine, standing behind the bar, her sandy blond hair pulled back in a ponytail. Her green eyes seemed to sparkle with an inner fire, a mixture of curiosity and determination that hinted at something far more than just a simple bartender.

"Found her," I said, nodding toward the bar. "Let's go."

With renewed purpose, I pushed my way through the throng of patrons, my friends following closely behind. The cacophony of voices and clinking glasses seemed to fade as I focused on the task ahead. Catherine, I hoped, held the key to finding Melanie and bringing her to justice.

The din of laughter and raucous conversation washed over me as I approached the bar, my heart hammering out a steady rhythm in my chest. Catherine stood with her back to the polished wooden counter, wiping down a glass with a white cloth while she engaged in conversation with a patron.

"Cat," I said, raising my voice above the clamor. Catherine's gaze flicked up toward me, her eyes narrowing slightly as she took in my appearance. "Apologies for interrupting, and for ducking out the other night on you, but we need your help."

"Help?" Her eyebrows rose, a hint of skepticism dancing in her eyes. She set the glass down on the counter and crossed her arms, clearly curious despite herself. "What kind of help are you looking for? Dancing lessons," she grinned "sounds like a line from this side of the bar."

"Nothing that much fun, we need information," I replied, swallowing the lump of nerves that threatened to rise in my throat. "We're tracking someone – a woman I'm sure you've heard of or seen, Melanie Lancaster. Despite her reputation here in the islands, she's dangerous and a thief, and it's important we find her before she can cause more harm."

Catherine's gaze shifted between me, Goose, and the others behind me, analyzing our expressions for any hint of deception. The tension in the air was palpable, our shared purpose weighing heavily on us. I understood the importance of my words in that moment.

"I inquired about you after our last encounter, and despite the protective nature of those around you, I learned that you have a keen awareness of everything happening in these islands, even in the private villas and resorts," I explained, maintaining a steady tone despite my inner doubts. "We don't want to cause trouble for you or anyone else, but we are determined to stop the violence caused by Melanie. Will you assist us?"

Catherine held my gaze for a long moment, her green eyes piercing mine with a predatory intensity. I met her stare with unwavering resolve, knowing that our mission hinged on her response.

"Okay," she finally said, her voice barely audible over the bar's din. "Let's discuss this further. I don't like it, but my instincts tell me you're sincere. And I'm well aware of Melanie's nefarious reputation."

Leaning in closer, I emphasized the urgency of our situation. "Time is of the essence, Cat," I urged in a hushed tone. "Every moment Melanie remains free is another opportunity for her to evade capture and harm innocent people."

Catherine glanced at my companions behind me, her expression contemplative. After a moment, she nodded slowly.

"Alright, Hutch," she murmured, her gaze returning to me. "I'll share what I've heard through the grapevine. People tend to overlook the barkeep and loosen their tongues at the bar, especially after a few drinks."

She proceeded to divulge information about Melanie's whereabouts, mentioning a villa and a private island called Sangre Key. As she spoke, I envisioned the remote island and the potential dangers it held. The thought of Melanie's schemes unfolding in such a secluded location sent a shiver down my spine.

"Thank you, Catherine," I expressed, a faint smile playing on my lips. "And by the way, it's hard to imagine anyone overlooking you."

She smiled, but her expression quickly turned serious but determined. "Just make sure that woman faces justice, Hutch. Ensure she can't harm anyone else. I know several people here who had investments in the power plant."

"I promise," I responded, my determination solidifying. We would track down Melanie and put an end to her destructive actions, no matter what it took. There was no alternative.

The room felt smaller as Catherine's words hung heavily in the air. My friends and I exchanged knowing glances, silently acknowledging the difficult road ahead. The background noise in the bar seemed distant compared to the ticking clock in my mind.

"Are you all ready for this?" I asked my friends, seeking reassurance that they were prepared for the challenges ahead.

"Absolutely," Goose affirmed, his gaze unwavering. "We're behind you, Hutch."

"Definitely," Jack added, his expression resolute.

"Okay then," I said, turning back to Catherine. "Cat, I hate to ask, but we could use your expertise if you're willing."

"Of course," she replied, her determination evident. "I may not be able to accompany you, but I can provide valuable information about Sangre Key."

"Thank you, Catherine," I said gratefully. As the weight of our mission settled on my shoulders, I knew her insights would be crucial in navigating the island and locating Melanie.

"Plus," Catherine continued, her eyes reflecting a shared determination, "I want to see that woman face justice just as much as you do."

"Then we'll collaborate to ensure that justice is served." Thoughts of plans and strategies raced through my mind, focusing on the logistics of reaching the island and apprehending Melanie. Amidst the chaos, a glimmer of hope emerged – a belief that together, we could bring an end to her destructive actions.

"Let's get to work," I declared firmly. Our journey had just begun, but we were prepared to confront whatever awaited us on Sangre Key – and to ensure that justice prevailed. The room buzzed with conversation and clinking glasses as I locked eyes with Catherine.

"We appreciate your assistance, Catherine. Your knowledge will be invaluable to our mission."

"Of course," she replied, her determination shining through. "But there's much to discuss – our travel plans, required resources, and the obstacles we may encounter on the island."

"Agreed, wait ... we?" I inquired, nodding as my mind raced with ideas and strategies. Goose and the rest of the group leaned in, fully engaged. We understood the magnitude of the task ahead.

"Yes, we ... Let's meet Payton tomorrow morning to finalize our plans," Catherine suggested, her gaze locked onto mine. I don't know what her reasons were but it was clear that she shared our sense of urgency and commitment to the mission.

"Sounds good," I replied, feeling a renewed sense of purpose. With Catherine on board, our odds of success increased exponentially, although a civilian also increased the complexity. "We'll see you here at first light."

"First light it is," Catherine confirmed, determination and resolve etched on her face.

As I turned back to my friends, I caught Goose's approving nod, his eyes conveying a silent message: This woman can help us, Hutch. She's got the fire in her, just like us.

"Alright, folks," I said, addressing the group. "Let's call it a night. Tomorrow, we begin our journey to Sangre Key."

"Here's to justice," Goose murmured, raising an imaginary glass in the air. The others echoed his sentiment, their faces a mix of steely resolve and quiet anticipation.

"Justice," I whispered to myself, feeling the weight of our responsibility settle firmly on my shoulders. As I stood amidst my friends and newfound ally, I knew we were ready to face whatever darkness lay ahead – together.

The following morning, well before sunrise and our meeting with Catherine, my team and I gathered around a sturdy wooden table, its surface smoothed by years of use and conversation. Spread out before us were maps and notes.

"Okay," I started, my voice firm and focused. "Catherine's information gives us a good lead on where Melanie might be. But reaching that island won't be easy, even with her connections there. She's taking care of arranging a boat, navigating dangerous waters, and preparing for any defenses Melanie might have in place."

"Hutch, I hate to say it, but we can't be sure about Catherine," Payton interjected, his eyes narrowed in thought. "She could be helpful or a hindrance, depending on her loyalties."

"Agreed," I admitted, rubbing my chin in contemplation. "But we don't have many options. We need her knowledge and contacts if we want to locate Melanie."

"Then we need to be prepared for anything," Goose added, his expression serious. "We have to be ready for the worst-case scenario, including being double-crossed."

Looking at my friends – my family – gathered around the table, I knew we were capable of seeing this mission through. Our bond was unbreakable, forged in the fires of adversity and fueled by our shared determination. Together, we would fight for justice, no matter the challenges we faced.

Chapter 8

"I firmly believe that any man's finest hour, the greatest fulfillment of all that he holds dear, is that moment when he has worked his heart out in a good cause and lies exhausted on the field of battle - victorious."

--Vince Lombardi

Catherine's contact successfully guided us to Sangre Key with efficiency and discretion. As we set out at dawn, the sound of our boots on the gravel path echoed through the tranquil beach, leading us into the untamed heart of the island. The salty tang of the sea lingered in the humid air, creating a sense of anticipation as we ventured deeper into the lush greenery. The only sounds were the distant calls of hidden birds, adding to the eerie stillness that surrounded us.

"Stay alert for any surveillance equipment," I cautioned, scanning the dense foliage. "And watch out for any potential threats, whether they be natural or man-made."

"It feels like we're walking into a dangerous situation," Gordo remarked, swatting at a pesky mosquito.

"It's better to be proactive than to wait for trouble to find us," Jack responded, his hand hovering near the S&W 5.7x28 pistol holstered at his side.

My attention was caught by the dense foliage, on the lookout for any signs of movement. The island was teeming with creatures that were not welcoming to outsiders. We were the intruders in their territory.

"Trust muscle memory," I reminded myself and the team. "Stay alert, stay alive."

The terrain became rough, the path narrowing to a mere game trail. Vines entangled our legs, and the air was heavy with the smell of decaying plants. A sudden downpour soaked the ground, turning it into mud. We pushed forward, rain pelting down on us, our determination keeping us going.

"Stay close, keep moving," I instructed, my voice barely audible over the rain. "We'll find shelter soon."

It wasn't just nature we were facing. Eyes watched us from the shadows, locals suspicious of strangers. Their whispers carried on the wind, a language unknown but filled with distrust. We were not welcome here, and they made sure we knew it.

"Let me handle the talking," Cat said as we encountered a group blocking our path. "We don't want any misunderstandings."

Approaching slowly with hands visible, Cat explained who we were and our purpose. Her tone was respectful, her words careful.

After a tense moment, they allowed us to pass. No smiles, no warmth, but no violence either. It was a small victory.

"Good job, Cat," Payton praised as we moved past the silent onlookers.

"Just doing my job," Cat replied, her gaze watchful. Every step forward was a step into the unknown.

"Hey, Hutch, how much farther?" Goose asked, sounding tired.

"We're nearing the area Cat's contact identified," I replied, leading the team deeper into the island. There was no turning back now. We were committed to this path, whatever dangers it held. I was determined to keep my team safe.

Crouching low, I scanned the foliage for any hidden threats. The atmosphere was heavy with humidity and the weight of our mission.

48

My fingers tapped against my thigh, a silent rhythm to calm my nerves. Then I heard a sound, unfamiliar in the jungle.

"Did you hear that? Gordo, keep an eye out from above, Goose, disrupt communications," I whispered, barely audible over the insect noise.

"Already working on it," Goose responded, his tone serious. He opened his durable laptop, a small piece of technology that seemed out of place in the rugged environment. His fingers swiftly typed on the keyboard, like a skilled pianist performing a high-stakes concerto.

"Give me two minutes," he said, and I understood not to rush him. Goose's expertise with electronics was renowned in our group. He had a talent for extracting information from technology like no one else I knew.

"Make it one," I replied calmly. Time was not just valuable; it was crucial for our survival.

"I'm disrupting their communications now," Goose announced a moment later, his voice filled with satisfaction. A series of clicks and tones emanated from his speakers, creating a symphony of interference. If anyone was eavesdropping on us, they would only hear static now.

"Great job," I praised him, watching as Goose nodded in satisfaction, his quick thinking proving invaluable once again.

"Okay, Gordo, your turn," I said, turning to our pilot.

"The drone is going up," Gordo stated calmly. With practiced ease, he launched a sleek quadcopter drone, its rotors humming loudly as it soared through the dense air. The drone's camera feed displayed a bird's-eye view on Gordo's tablet screen, revealing the jungle below us like a living organism.

"It looks clear for the next half-mile," Gordo reported, his voice steady, unaffected by the adrenaline pumping through my veins. "But

49

there's a clearing up ahead—likely man-made. That's probably where that noise came from."

"Lead the way," I instructed, pointing to the image on the screen.

We moved quietly, following the drone's guidance. Every sound seemed amplified, every movement in the undergrowth felt like a warning of unseen dangers. But we pressed on, driven by the need to find Melanie and uncover the mystery she had left behind.

"Wait," Gordo suddenly interrupted, halting us in our tracks. "There's movement. It's not wildlife." He zoomed in on the tablet screen, revealing a group of figures moving stealthily through the terrain parallel to ours.

"Melanie's mercenaries, I would assume," I whispered, recognizing their disciplined stride and tactical gear similar to ours. Goose looked at me, his brown eyes filled with determination.

"It's time to change course," I decided, placing complete trust in Gordo's gathered information. We couldn't risk a confrontation just yet. We needed to be fully prepared, with all the advantages on our side.

"Gordo suggested taking the path to the right to avoid their path and prevent them from detecting us," Gordo advised, his focus fixed on the screen.

"Let's go," I ordered, my mind racing with plans, contingencies, and potential outcomes. We moved silently, like ghosts among the foliage, guided by our surveillance drone and the quick thinking of my team.

Each step we took was a silent promise—a commitment to seeking justice for what had been done, and a determination to face the consequences head-on, no matter how severe. This island, with its hidden dangers and wild beauty, was just another test. And we were the ones being tested.

As soon as we returned to our original path on solid ground, trouble found us once more. Figures emerged from the dense jungle—mercenaries, their intentions clear in the cold glint of their weapons and the calculated precision of their approach.

"Move!" I yelled, each word a command that brought order to the chaos. They assessed us, weighing their options in a deadly game where lives were the stakes. But they underestimated us, mistaking us for local law enforcement or something worse. They hadn't anticipated facing a team forged in the fires of countless battles fought together.

"Goose, Jack, flank left. Gordo, Payton, right. Take the high ground." My instructions were swift, the plan unfolding in my mind—a choreography of movements and counter-movements, a strategic dance on the battlefield.

I led the way, standing firm, my body a shield for the rest of the team as they positioned themselves. The mercenaries hesitated, unsure of who to follow, their uncertainty reflected in their eyes, while our determination spoke a language they understood all too well.

"Stand down! Whatever she is paying you is useless if you're not alive to spend it." I shouted, my voice as firm as bedrock. This wasn't a battle of bullets but of wills, a clash not just of arms but of convictions. And mine was an unwavering fortress built from duty, honor, and a promise to seek justice for the shadows Melanie cast upon us all.

The standoff lingered, a tense wire humming with the potential for violence. But amidst the focus, my mind replayed every decision that led us here, every consequence we bore like Atlas under the weight of the world.

Then, as if a silent signal passed among them, the mercenaries retreated, slipping back into the jungle's embrace. We had triumphed in this round, not through force, but through the sheer indomitable will of a team united in purpose.

"Good job," I whispered, though my commendation was unnecessary. These men of valor and vigor knew their value, my brothers-in-arms bound by more than mere mission. Together, we pressed forward, drawing nearer to Melanie, to the heart of the labyrinth she ensnared us in. Consequences awaited at its core, a reckoning that murmured through the leaves, assuring that justice, however elusive, would not elude us.

As if on cue, the sky darkened ominously, the clouds swirling into a menacing grey as we navigated through the underbrush, the air heavy with the scent of an impending storm. Goose's eyes flicked from his tablet to the sky; his expression tight. "Gordo, is the drone still operational? If so, bring it down," he cautioned. "Radar picked up a massive thunderstorm heading our way. We need to find some shelter."

"Over there!" Gordo gestured towards a rocky outcrop he had spotted with the drone that offered some cover. I took the lead, urging the team towards the outcropping. The wind howled, a piercing cry threatening to uproot the trees. We clustered together beneath the stone, our bodies a shield against the relentless onslaught.

As the tempest raged, I contemplated the parallels between the storm's chaos and the turmoil Melanie had unleashed in our lives—both were uncontrollable forces, leaving destruction in their wake. But here, amidst nature's fury, we stood united, our determination solidifying like the rocks that shielded us.

When the downpour subsided, we emerged to a world cleansed, the jungle alive and glistening with moisture. In the aftermath, Gordo sent the drone back up, its blades cutting through the damp air. Through the lens of technology, we sought clarity.

"Guys, you need to see this," Gordo's voice crackled over the walkie-talkie, a hint of excitement in his usual calm demeanor. We gathered around the small screen attached to the controller in his hands, observing as the drone hovered over a clearing. There, hidden among the foliage, was a structure—modern, out of place, and undeniably conspicuous.

"Melanie always did love the dramatic," I remarked, studying the building that seemed to mock us with its presence.

"Looks like she's playing queen of the jungle," Payton joked, though his gaze was resolute.

"Let's not keep her waiting then," I declared, feeling the familiar surge of adrenaline, the instinct of the hunter to pursue the prey. This was more than a clue; it was a beckoning call, leading us towards the inevitable confrontation. "Jack, set up a rotation. I want surveillance on that compound at all times. I've requested a few more reinforcements to be dropped in. The five of us and Cat, as skilled as she is, simply don't have the numbers."

"Hutch, love you man, but we just trekked for nearly 10 hours to get here. How are you bringing in more people tonight?" Goose inquired, curiosity evident on his face.

I chuckled, partly because I anticipated the question and partly due to the expression on his face. "It's simple. First, we weren't certain of our destination, but now we are. Second, I reached out to someone even crazier than Crazy Train. Brother Jeremy and a couple of his buddies are HALO'ing in."

"Hell, Brother J makes me seem normal," Payton chimed in with a smile.

Goose, Gordo, and Jack all nodded in agreement with Payton's observation.

53

With that, we began planning and preparing, each of us lost in our thoughts but united by the common purpose that connected us. Melanie had woven a web of deceit and cunning, but we were not mere prey to be ensnared. We were the hunters closing in, armed with resilience and unity. As the shadows grew longer, we moved forward, our footsteps a silent promise of justice yet to be served.

We settled in a small clearing as dusk descended, casting the jungle in twilight hues. I activated the IR beacon to guide Jeremy and his team to our location. The adrenaline that had fueled our actions now faded, leaving us in a collective silence. I leaned against a gnarled tree, surveying the faces of the men I trusted with more than just my life. In this moment of respite, their weary yet determined expressions told a story of courage and camaraderie.

"Remember when we thought this was going to be a vacation?" Goose's question broke the silence, laced with irony. A soft chuckle rippled through the group, briefly lightening the gravity of our situation.

Suddenly, a figure emerged from the trees like a phantom, "Feels like a lifetime ago," a booming voice declared, flipping through an old Bible. I recognized Jeremy immediately, his unwavering faith evident in the worn Bible he carried. His presence was a beacon of steadfastness in the darkness.

"Damn, Brother, you just scared a few years off my life. How did you manage to sneak up on us like that? I must be losing my touch," I remarked, my heart racing.

Jeremy chuckled, his calm demeanor soothing our nerves, "With these ocean breezes, we were already past your location when we spotted the beacon. We landed in the clearing to the east and hiked over here."

"It's good to have you with us, brother. Every step we take brings us closer to bringing Melanie to justice," Jack affirmed, his blue eyes reflecting the fire's glow, a symbol of determination in the encroaching darkness. His steady presence anchored us against the storm of uncertainty.

I nodded, feeling the weight of our shared mission and the strength found in our unity. "Jeremy, meet my team," I introduced with handshakes all around. "And this is Catherine, our guide and a skilled bartender. She's the reason we're not lost in Nassau chasing our tails," I added.

As Jeremy and his team settled in and received the full briefing from the rest of us, I couldn't help but reflect on our newest member, Brother Jeremy McGuinness. His unique combination of faith and warrior spirit made him an indispensable part of our team, and he was truly one of the most mysterious individuals I had ever served alongside.

"Hey Hutch," Catherine inquired, her eyes showing a hint of curiosity. "Can you share more about this Machine Gun Preacher, Jeremy? How did you two meet?" Her question brought me back to the present moment.

"Brother Jeremy is truly one-of-a-kind," I began, my voice filled with admiration. "I first crossed paths with him on a mission trip to Rwanda with Empowerment through Entrepreneurship, a charity that I established to mentor young entrepreneurs. He was a preacher with a military background similar to mine, and he's also a successful entrepreneur who has launched multiple thriving businesses."

"A mission trip and you a charity founder? That's unexpected... but it sounds like a fortunate encounter," Catherine commented, raising her eyebrows.

"His faith drives his actions, and like many of us on the team, he has witnessed the darker aspects of humanity firsthand and understands the necessity of combating them," I continued, recalling the times Jeremy had stood by our side in battle. "He is both

55

compassionate and unwavering in his pursuit of justice. When the going gets tough, he's the person you want on your side."

Catherine nodded thoughtfully, clearly impressed by my portrayal of our enigmatic comrade.

"His presence has always been a source of strength for us," I admitted, feeling grateful for the strong bond that united us. "We've faced numerous challenges together, and he has never faltered in his dedication to our cause or his faith."

"He sounds like a valuable asset to the team," she remarked appreciatively. "I'm glad he's part of our group."

"Believe me, whether you're battling an external foe or your inner demons, you won't find a better friend or ally than Brother Jeremy," I affirmed, my words carrying a deep sense of certainty.

With renewed determination, we continued forward, guided by the unbreakable bonds of friendship and our shared mission for justice. No matter what dangers lay ahead, we would face them together – a united front that could not be easily overcome.

In the quiet of the moment, our rest was both physical and, thanks to Jeremy, spiritual, offering a brief respite from the turmoil. We were warriors fighting for what was right, each carrying the scars of battles past and those yet to come. But tonight, we were connected by something stronger than blood—a commitment sealed with loyalty and the unspoken assurance that none of us would walk this path alone.

As the night grew darker and the jungle whispered its secrets, we began to prepare for our mission. The tension inside me coiled like a spring, anticipation building for our 3:00am operation, filled with the promise of conflict and, hopefully, resolution.

"Let's check our gear," Hutch finally spoke, his voice taking on a commanding tone. We moved efficiently, inspecting our weapons, securing supplies, ensuring we were ready for any scenario. The drone was poised, ready to reveal the mysteries hidden in the shadows.

"It's time to put an end to this," Payton declared, his words cutting through the air, his fearless demeanor enveloping us like a shield.

As we readied ourselves to depart, I felt the predator within me awaken, senses heightened by the nearness of our target. We were a team, a unit forged in the crucible of adversity and strengthened by our pursuit of justice. This was more than just seeking revenge; it was a statement of consequence—a declaration that every action had a reaction.

And so, we ventured into the night, a pack of wolves disguised as humans, our gaze fixed on the horizon and the storm brewing beyond. We were prepared.

Chapter 9

"In order to achieve good, one may need to confront evil."

--Robert McNamara

As we moved cautiously through the dense foliage, the sound of heavy boots crunching twigs sent a jolt of tension through us. Melanie Lancaster, known as The Siren, had escalated the stakes; we were no longer dealing with a mere con artist. She had surrounded herself with ruthless mercenaries, men who moved with deadly precision and loyalty to her cause.

"Spread out," I communicated quietly through our comms, every word deliberate and controlled. We had anticipated resistance, but Gordo's drone revealed a large number of heavily armed guards patrolling the area.

"Get down!!" Gordo's urgent shout alerted us to imminent danger. We took cover as bullets whizzed past, the adrenaline pumping through our veins. This was no longer a simple retrieval mission; it had turned into a fight for survival. Jack, always the strategist, signaled a flanking maneuver with swift and precise hand gestures in the darkness.

"Wait for my signal," he whispered, as shadows closed in on our position.

We had prepared for this moment, trained for it, and when the time came, instinct took over. My hand found the grip of my Styer AUG as if guided by some unseen force, and my aim was steady. Gunfire erupted, cutting through the night with deadly accuracy, and for a brief moment, we moved as one in a chaotic dance of necessity.

Move! Three o'clock, 200 meters," Gordo's voice crackled over the comms, and we obeyed, darting between trees, boots skidding on loose earth. They were professional, these hired guns of Melanie's, better than I would have guessed she had access to, but they were a patchwork of men, whereas we were a tempest honed by years of shoulder-to-shoulder combat.

In the brief lulls, I caught glimpses of Payton barreling forward, fearless as ever, drawing fire and dishing out retribution with equal fervor. His courage was a beacon, rallying us even as doubt tried to claw its way into our minds.

"Keep pushing!" Jack's command cut through the cacophony. We advanced, exploiting weaknesses with practiced precision, covering each other's backs. We were a singular entity, each of us a gear in a well-oiled machine built on trust and an unspoken promise to see this through, regardless of the cost.

As dawn began to spill its light on the scene of our skirmish, we regrouped, chests heaving, eyes alert. We had driven them back and reduced their numbers to match ours, but we also knew it was likely only a brief reprieve. Melanie's mercenaries would return, likely in greater numbers.

"Next time, they won't be so lucky," I muttered, knowing full well that we could be the unlucky ones as well. But as I looked around at my comrades, their faces set with grim determination, I felt a surge of confidence. Together, there was nothing we couldn't face—even the ruthless protectors of The Siren's dark ambitions.

Moments later, bullets whizzed past, kicking up debris where they kissed the ground. Dust swirled around us, a shroud for our movements as we ducked behind a crumbling wall, the echo of gunfire our relentless adversary. With each shot, my heart hammered in time—a fierce drumbeat calling us to action.

"Goose, we need an edge," I called out, my voice steady despite the adrenaline coursing through my veins. The mercenaries' coordination was clearly practiced, and their tactics were disciplined.

It was clear Melanie had invested heavily in her guardians, and it would cost us dearly if we didn't adapt—and fast.

"Already on it, Hutch," Goose replied, fingers dancing over the portable device he'd pulled from his pack. His brow furrowed in concentration, the corners of his mouth twitching with the ghost of a smirk. I knew that look—it was the silent herald of his ingenuity at work.

"Keep their heads down as long as we can," I instructed the others, peeking over our cover to assess the enemy's formation. A tactical puzzle lay before us, one I intended to solve. Each piece had to be maneuvered precisely, and every move was calculated. Lives depended on it—our lives.

I observed Goose silently celebrating as a chorus of confused shouts erupted from our opponents. Goose had successfully compromised their communications, leaving them disoriented and vulnerable.

"Move, now!" I commanded, cutting through the chaos. We surged forward, taking advantage of the momentary confusion. With their communications down, whoever had been providing them with information about our movements was no longer a threat; the mercenaries were slower to react, their coordinated movements disrupted by our strategic chaos.

"Keep them off balance, Hutch," Goose said, a glint in his eye as he continued to disrupt their communications. His hands moved quickly, his focus unwavering. In the digital age, Goose wielded technology like a skilled swordsman, cutting through the enemy's defenses with precision.

"Flank left—advance!" I ordered, navigating the battlefield with precision. With each command, we whittled down their numbers, taking advantage of the confusion caused by Goose's electronic skills.

We pressed forward with determination, knowing we had regained the advantage. As the dust settled and the gunfire subsided, I took a moment to catch my breath. Our enemies were scattered, but not yet defeated.

"Great job," I acknowledged Goose, giving him a pat on the back. "You saved us."

"Anytime, Hutch," he replied, his smile contagious. However, our celebration was short-lived as we faced the harsh reality of our situation.

Melanie has evolved from a simple con artist committing investment fraud to a more serious player. I pondered aloud, scanning the horizon for any potential threats. We still had work to do, but together, we were a formidable team.

The quietness around us was deceptive, hinting at the storm that was about to hit. Through Gordo's drone, we could see the world in sharp detail, analyzing every movement and shadow for hidden dangers

"Big Brother is watching," Gordo whispered, expertly controlling the drone. It flew above us silently, transmitting crucial information to our command center.

"Any sign of the remaining mercenaries who escaped?" I asked calmly, despite the adrenaline coursing through me.

"No, the area is clear up to 5 kilometers, for now," he replied. "But stay alert. I'm concerned about possible tunnels."

His composure calmed me, providing stability in the chaos. Trusting in his vigilance, I turned to Jack, who was poised and focused on the horizon.

"Jack," I acknowledged his readiness. "Any thoughts?"

"Check the perimeter. Keep rotations tight," he responded immediately. "Don't give them any room to maneuver."

"Agreed," I nodded, appreciating his strategic insight. Jack's instructions were clear and concise, a reflection of his military precision.

"Movement, southeast ridge!" Gordo suddenly alerted us. We all tensed, ready to act. I strained to see in the indicated direction, but my eyes couldn't match the drone's vision.

"Three... no, two hostiles. Armed with heavy rifles," Gordo reported calmly, providing us with crucial information. "They seem to be trying to flank us."

"Damn," I muttered quietly. "Let's go. Jack, what's the plan?"

"Two by two cover. Close-quarters engagement," Jack directed, and we moved in unison, our movements well-practiced.

As we advanced, Jack's hand signals guided us efficiently. We moved as a cohesive unit, each member following Jack's lead.

"Split on my signal..." Jack whispered, barely audible in the silence.

"The drone is watching your back," Gordo reassured us, focused on controlling the drone.

"Three... two... one... Go!"

Like a dam bursting, we surged forward with lethal intent. Gordo's live feed streamed directly into our earpieces, providing crucial updates that painted a more accurate picture than we could see with our own eyes.

"Left flank, advance. Right, hold. Enemy retreating to..." Gordo's voice trailed off, his tone changing. "Wait. Something's not right."

"Talk to me, Gordo," I said, feeling my pulse quicken.

"Signals are being jammed. They have tech—" His warning was interrupted by static.

"Comms compromised," Jack stated. "We're going old school."

We reverted to basic communication methods: hand signals, eye contact, and subtle nods. Jack's unspoken commands guided us through the firefight as if nothing had changed.

Bullets whistled past as we maneuvered, but Jack's foresight had positioned us advantageously. Every shot was deliberate, every move purposeful, our trust in each other our greatest strength.

"Push through!" Jack's voice cut through the static, clear and resolute. And we did, facing the onslaught with determination, knowing that together, we were stronger than as individuals.

As the gunfire subsided, we regrouped, checking for injuries. Our enemies had underestimated us once again and paid the price. They assumed disrupting our comms would cause confusion, but they were mistaken.

"Status?" I asked, surveying my team.

"Intact," Jack confirmed, reloading his weapon with precision.

The team checked in, all a bit battered but mostly unharmed from the intense battle.

"Drone's down, but I have backups," Gordo mentioned, undeterred by the setback.

"Good," I said, feeling the weight of responsibility. "Let's keep moving. Melanie's presence out here is close—I can sense it."

We pressed on, the taste of victory mixed with apprehension as we approached the looming threat. With my tactics, Jack's leadership, Goose and Gordo's tech expertise, and the team's diverse skills, we were a formidable force—a truth solidified in our determination and unity.

Chapter 10

"The enemy of my enemy is my friend."

-- ancient proverb

The sound of the drone faded as we advanced further into the forest, each step deliberate and precise. The rush of adrenaline from the recent firefight still lingered, a reminder of the high stakes of our mission. The darkness seemed to conceal potential dangers, every shadow a possible threat.

"Stay alert," I murmured over the comms, my voice barely audible. "We're not in the clear yet."

I moved closer, the scent of gunpowder lingering in the air, and peered over his shoulder.

Gordo's response came through the comms, composed and clear. "Copy that, Hutch. Scanning the perimeter with thermal. The dense foliage is obstructing my visual."

We continued forward in silence, our footsteps muffled by the forest floor. Moonlight filtered through the thick canopy above, creating eerie patterns on the ground. Jack led the way, his instincts sharp and commanding, guiding us without a word.

As we neared the edge of the forest, a clearing came into view. In the center stood an old, abandoned building, a relic of the past with crumbling walls and vines creeping through broken windows. This was the location Gordo had pointed us to, a potential stronghold linked to Melanie's operations.

"Keep an eye on the building," Payton whispered, his voice tense. "No visible guards, but we can't assume it's safe."

"Understood," I nodded, gesturing for the team to spread out and approach cautiously. "Gordo, maintain drone surveillance. We need to watch for any unexpected activity."

64

"Got it," he confirmed, monitoring the drone's feed for any signs of movement. "Thermals show minimal activity inside. Could be well insulated or a trap."

"Let's find out," Jack muttered, tightening his grip on his weapon. "Time to move."

We advanced in unison, moving with precision and purpose. As we drew closer to the building, I spotted a shadow moving inside, alerting the team.

"Hold," I signaled, halting our progress. "We have company."

The team paused, on high alert as we waited for any further signs of movement. A voice came over the comms, breaking the silence.

"Goose, what do you see?" I asked, keeping my eyes on the figure inside.

"Yeah," he responded, typing rapidly. "This isn't what we expected. I'm hacking into their system now to access security cameras."

"We need eyes inside," I stated, feeling the tension rise.

After a few moments, Goose reported his success in accessing the security feed, allowing us to see the interior of the building. The figure inside moved purposefully, unaware of our presence.

"It looks like they're setting up a data center," Gordo observed. "Possibly a communication hub."

"Then we need to take it down," Jack declared, his tone resolute. "Let's secure the building and gather intel."

"Agreed," I replied as we prepared to move in.

We entered the building together, moving stealthily through the broken entrance and into the complex interior. The air inside was musty, heavy with the smell of decay. We proceeded cautiously, checking each room for any potential threats. A shadowy figure reappeared, a lone guard patrolling the corridors.

"Payton, take care of him," I commanded in a low voice.

Crazy Train nodded and disappeared into the shadows. Shortly after, a soft thud indicated the guard had been taken out. We continued on, the eerie silence of the building surrounding us.

We eventually reached the central room, filled with old equipment and stacks of papers. In the middle, on a new raised floor, were multiple server racks containing various networking devices. Gordo and Goose got to work, connecting their devices to the hub.

"Just give me a minute," Gordo muttered, focused on his task.

As Goose searched through the digital archives, Gordo set up a relay to monitor the incoming data. The rest of us secured the area, keeping watch for any potential threats. Time passed slowly, testing our patience and determination.

"Jackpot," Goose finally announced, a smile on his face. "I've found their files. This place was indeed a relay station for their communications. We should be able to trace their signals back to the main hub."

"Great job," I praised, patting him on the shoulder. "Download everything quickly. We need to move fast, as I'm sure we've triggered an offsite alarm."

As Goose transferred the data, I looked at my team, their faces showing determination. We were a formidable force, battle-hardened and ready to take down Melanie Lancaster's empire.

With the data secured, we left the building and returned to the forest, moving swiftly and quietly. The first light of dawn was breaking, illuminating the landscape. We headed to our extraction point, where a helicopter was waiting. The pilot was likely surprised, as I had booked the flight as a sightseeing tour. Luckily, Catherine was able to persuade him to keep quiet.

As we boarded the helicopter, I glanced back at the abandoned building, a silent witness to our mission. Melanie's reign was coming to an end, and we were prepared for the final showdown in this unfolding saga.

The sun was setting, casting long shadows in the war room we had set up in an old shipping container on the docks in Nassau. Papers, maps, and digital screens covered the space, each one a piece of Melanie Lancaster's puzzle. I was studying nautical charts, tracing ancient trade routes, while the team examined the artifacts of her deception.

"Check this out," I said, pointing to a folder of information we had printed from Melanie's files. "A complete history and dossier on The Isabella. Lost in 1756, rumored to be carrying gold bound for Spain."

"Melanie always had expensive tastes," Payton joked from the corner, his eyes on the dossier. His attempt at humor was overshadowed by the seriousness of our mission.

"More than just taste," I replied. "Greed. The kind that doesn't care about collateral damage."

The Isabella had surfaced in Melanie's decrypted files. It became clear that her investment fraud was a way to fund the search for the lost treasure of The Isabella.

"Guys, come see this," Goose called out. We gathered around his station, where he had hacked into a satellite feed.

"I decrypted more of Melanie's files," he said, his fingers moving quickly. "She's been tracking deep-sea salvage operations and historical shipwrecks worldwide."

"Confirming our suspicions," I said, feeling the pieces fall into place. The ancient shipwreck was her goal; the scam was just a means to fund it. I suspected she learned about the Isabella from her college roommate, Kate Banister.

Kate, a marine archeologist, had helped us with a shipwreck off the coast of Texas in the past.

"And here's the twist," Goose said, zooming in on coordinates. "She's narrowed down the Isabella's location to a 10-square-mile area. And she has a salvage team there already."

"Her ambition knows no bounds," Jack muttered. "The treasure from that wreck would make her untouchable."

"Or finance a small army," Payton added, frowning.

"Either way, we can't allow that fortune to end up in her possession, not to mention the fact that she'll obliterate any history stored on that wreck," I declared, my determination solidifying like steel. This was more than just recovering stolen riches—it was about preventing a surge of power from landing in Melanie's lap.

"Goose, any information on her security measures?" I inquired, fully aware of the potential resistance we might encounter.

"Working on it," he responded, his focus fixed on the screen. "She's using top-notch encryption, but I'll crack it given time."

"We don't have the luxury of time." My hand instinctively touched the brim of my hat, silently seeking the insight we required.

Gordo suggested, Goose, what about contacting Cyrus? He..."

"WTF? Cyrus Marque? Are you serious," Goose interjected loudly. "That guy's just as bad as Melanie. You know our history."

Gordo raised his hands in an attempt to defuse the situation. "I understand your history and share your dislike for Cyrus, but he also despises Melanie intensely. She betrayed him when she was caught back in the States and tried to blame everything on him. He may be a criminal, but he's familiar with her connections."

Listening to the conversation and absorbing it all, I added, "Goose, there's merit in the saying 'the enemy of my enemy is my friend.'"

"Damn it and damn her," Goose retorted.

Gordo began to respond, but I subtly raised a hand. I had known Goose since fourth grade and understood that he was processing the options and facts at lightning speed.

After what seemed like an eternity, Goose relented, "Okay, setting aside emotions, you're right. If it helps bring Melabitch to justice, I can swallow my pride, hold my nose, and try to locate Cyrus."

"Thank you, Goose," I said, patting him on the shoulder. "Every bit of information could give us the advantage we need. We need to be aware of what we're facing out there." I watched him nod, already immersed in a whirlwind of emotions and choices—a whirlwind I trusted him to navigate.

I turned back to the map, the vast ocean staring back at me. It was no longer just a body of water but a battleground where the clash between right and wrong would unfold. Where hidden secrets and dangers lurked in the depths, and where the repercussions of our actions would extend far beyond the horizon. We were in the midst of the storm, but we were prepared to ride the waves.

Chapter 11

"We need a common enemy to unite us."

-- Condoleezza Rice

The room was filled with a stale air, heavy with the scent of old metal and unwashed bodies. I observed from a distance, my gaze fixed on Goose as he made his way through the underground market. Depending on who you asked, this place was either a hacker's paradise or a nightmare. I couldn't help but wonder if Goose felt a sense of pride or pity for how far Cyrus had fallen, my thoughts interrupted by the sight of Goose's old rival—Cyrus Marque, at a booth hidden in shadows.

"Black," Cyrus spoke, his voice cutting through the background noise of quiet conversations and electronic beeps. "Didn't think they allowed your kind in these parts."

"Marque," Goose responded, his tone steady. "I see you're still selling subpar hacks."

The tension between them crackled like electricity, sharp and unforgiving. Their shared history was marked by competition and betrayal—a history that began when they were teammates in the military. Cyrus smirked, exuding the confidence of a predator in his domain, while Goose stood firm, a reminder of past conflicts.

"Have you come to admit that I'm superior and seek assistance?" Cyrus taunted, leaning casually against the makeshift counter.

Let's just say I can acknowledge that in this particular case, you have inside information on how to obtain the information we need. You can enter through the front door, and I don't have the time to find a way to sneak in the back," Goose said, his gaze fixed on Cyrus. The challenge hung in the air, unspoken but understood.

"Why would I assist the man responsible for my expulsion from the military and the revocation of all my credentials? What's in it for me?" Cyrus inquired.

I interjected, informing Cyrus, "You were the cause of that. You chose to break the law for your own benefit, not Goose. As for what's in it for you... it's simple, payback. Melanie played a much larger role in shaping your current situation than anyone else."

Cyrus subtly nodded in agreement with my words, acknowledging that I was correct.

"Fine. Goose, take a seat and let's get started."

And so it commenced, a high-stakes game of chess played at a rapid pace. Each move and countermove brought them closer to their objective, but neither backed down. This wasn't just about determining who was the superior hacker; it was personal, a clash of egos and beliefs.

Despite the animosity, there was a begrudging recognition of each other's skills. They were two sides of the same coin, molded by their decisions, defined by their abilities. In this shadowy world where danger lurked in every bit, that acknowledgment was as close to respect as they would ever come.

The screens illuminated the dim room like twin beacons, casting an otherworldly glow on their faces. Their fingers moved swiftly across the keyboards, a flurry of activity that masked the tension between them.

"Melanie has something significant planned," Cyrus stated abruptly, his gaze fixed on the screen. "Something bigger than your team can handle."

I narrowed my eyes, noting the change in their demeanor. "You're not playing both sides, are you?"

Cyrus scoffed, a quick exhale through his nose. "As you're aware, I'm committed to seeing The Siren's downfall."

Goose encouraged Cyrus to reveal the information, his voice calm yet urgent. This wasn't just any hack; it was valuable intel that could make a difference in the game. Cyrus hesitated before sharing the coordinates and time – midnight – but admitted he wasn't sure what to expect. Goose pressed for more details, emphasizing the importance of information. Cyrus acknowledged his limitations but defended his efforts in providing the information quickly.

Goose reluctantly agreed, recognizing the power of even a small lead.

Jack noted the time constraint and distance to cover, emphasizing the need for a swift and discreet plan.

Gordo agreed, already strategizing for the mission ahead. The team prepared to leave, with Gordo setting a tight timeline for departure. They were determined to act swiftly and decisively, ready to turn obstacles into opportunities. The team's resolve was palpable, united in their pursuit of justice and retribution. They were prepared for whatever challenges lay ahead."

Chapter 12

"Anticipation of consequences is a key aspect of wisdom."

--Norman Cousins

Five hours later, the drone's rotors sliced through the salty air as Gordo skillfully piloted the craft over the rolling waves. From my spot on the deck, I could see the blinking light of the drone against the fading twilight sky. Gordo's movements were precise and practiced, guiding our eyes in the sky.

"Sea and deck are clear, no sentries in sight," Gordo reported calmly. The live feed from the drone painted a picture of Melanie's last known location—a cargo ship anchored a few miles away.

"Keep it low and let's see what we can learn from this ship," I instructed, studying the display over Gordo's shoulder.

Gordo nodded, a small smile playing on his lips as he maneuvered the drone closer to the waterline. The drone revealed a hidden hatch near the ship's stern—a potential entry point for us.

"Nice find," I noted, storing the information for later use. "Any heat signatures?"

"Switching to thermal now." The screen changed, showing heat signatures of guards and a mysterious source in the cargo hold. "There's something unusual in the cargo hold, could be what we're looking for."

"Could also be a trap," I cautioned.

"Agreed, but we need to investigate," Gordo replied, and I knew he was right.

As Gordo continued to survey the area, I turned to Jack, who had been quietly observing the operation, his blue eyes missing nothing.

The map laid out before us was dotted with notes and symbols, each a testament to my and Jack's meticulous planning.

"Based on Gordo's intel, we've got a few options," Jack began, tapping a finger against a circled area on the map. His demeanor was as solid as the deck beneath our feet, every word measured, every possibility considered.

"Frontal assault is a no-go—too exposed, too risky," he continued. The lines on his face deepened as he traced routes with his finger, plotting our course through a minefield of danger. "But that hatch Gordo found might just be our ticket in. We'd need to move under cover of darkness, keep it quiet."

"Split into teams?" I suggested trying to envision the plan coming together.

"Exactly. One team will create a diversion on the water and draw out as many of her people as possible. The other to slip in unnoticed, secure the target," Jack explained, his strategy unfolding with clinical precision.

"Risks?" I asked, knowing full well every choice here teetered on a knife's edge.

"Plenty," he admitted without hesitation. "Timing has to be perfect. Coordination is key. And if we're spotted …"

"Let's make sure we're not, then," I interjected, the weight of command settling onto my shoulders. "We'll need to use the rebreathers instead of scuba to avoid a bubble trail. Gordo, can you keep the drone airborne during the op for real-time updates?"

"Can do," Gordo replied confidently, never taking his eyes off the controls. "I'll have Goose set up a secondary feed so I can monitor both. We won't miss a beat."

"Alright," I said, clapping my hands together once, the sound sharp in the still evening air. "Let's prep for a night move. Everyone knows their role. It's time to bring Melanie's game to an end."

The group nodded, a silent orchestra tuning for the performance of their lives. Danger lurked in the shadows, but we were ready to dance with it, to bend it to our will. Justice was our partner, and together, we'd step onto the floor when night fell, moving in unison towards a conclusion written in the stars—or perhaps, in the dark waters where a shipwreck lay waiting with its secrets clenched tight.

"Remember," I emphasized, making eye contact with each of them, "Melanie doesn't follow the rules. Be prepared for anything. Watch each other's backs."

"Always," Gordo muttered, a faint smile playing on his lips.

"Then let's go," I stated, the seriousness of the situation weighing heavily on us like the night air.

We stood up together, a united group driven by a common goal and sharp instincts. Quietly, we dispersed into the night, ready to face the chaos that awaited us and dismantle Melanie's deceitful plans piece by piece.

Tonight, we were enforcers of justice, determined to thwart her elaborate, malicious schemes.

The sound of the motorboat's engine cut through the silence of the night, creating a steady rhythm. I checked my watch, glancing from the glowing hands to the equipment laid out in front of us with precision. Night vision goggles, grappling hooks, and an assortment of firearms glistened under the bright light of our makeshift base.

"Check comms," I whispered, adjusting the earpiece snug against my ear.

"Five-by-five, Hutch," each team member responded in my ear, unwavering. Gordo gave a thumbs-up from his post, surrounded by screens and keyboards that rivaled a mission control center. Even Jeremy, typically armed only with his faith and a pistol, inspected his weapon with practiced skill.

"Remember, keep in mind that we're uncertain about who or what we're up against, so use non-lethal force if possible. Our objective is not revenge, so adhere to rules of engagement by responding proportionally but decisively to any threats," I reminded them, the weight of leadership settling on me like a cloak.

"Understood," they echoed.

I pulled on my gloves, the familiar leather flexing easily with each movement. The others followed suit, their actions synchronized without a word spoken. Years of trust translated into silent understanding.

"Goose, are you confident about the signal jammer?" I inquired, eyeing the array of technology.

"As sure as the tide, Hutch. Once we activate it, they won't be able to send a message," he assured, his confidence evident.

"Good." I turned my gaze outside, where Gordo was launching his drone into the dark sky—a silent sentinel providing us with surveillance.

"Two minutes!" Goose called out, his voice resonating.

"Let's get ready," I said, pulling my tactical vest over my head. Pockets filled with essential tools, it hugged my body snugly, a second skin for the impending mission.

Jack walked beside me a reassuring presence. Payton donned a dark hood, blending into the shadows with expert stealth.

"Ready, preacher?" I asked, giving Jeremy a pat on the shoulder.

"Always," he replied, his steely gaze unwavering.

With that, Jeremy and his team boarded the RIB. As they departed, skimming the waves on the opposite side of the ship, we approached from our side.

The cargo ship loomed ahead, a dark silhouette against the starlit sky. My heart raced, adrenaline pumping through me, heightened senses on alert.

"Secure yourselves," I instructed, and the deck buzzed with activity as we fastened our gear.

"Thirty seconds," I announced, checking my Suunto dive computer for the time. The ship came into view through the darkness.

"Remember our purpose," I said, voice low but firm. "For those who have suffered injustice. For righteousness."

Heads nodded in agreement, a silent vow reaffirmed.

"Ten seconds."

"Go!" I shouted as the first firework exploded above the ocean. Jeremy's team had set up a series of fireworks to distract the enemy, giving us time to board the ship.

We quickly climbed the ropes and entered the ship within three minutes. The ship enveloped us as we moved deeper inside.

Tension built as we moved forward, knowing that the moment of truth was approaching. The answers we sought were ahead of us, and we were prepared for the final showdown.

As the last firework faded, the only sound was the echo of our footsteps on the deck. We moved forward as a united team, ready for the ultimate challenge that lay ahead.

Chapter 13

"Experience is the key to making good decisions, and sometimes that experience comes from making bad ones."

– Mark Twain

The ship's cargo hold was a maze of shadows and echoes, filled with the scent of salt and rust. Our flashlights pierced the darkness, revealing stacks of crates and barrels, their labels faded and unreadable. Gordo's drone hovered nearby, casting a eerie light as we carefully searched the area.

"What exactly are we looking for?" Payton's voice came through the comms, a mix of curiosity and tension.

"Anything that connects Melanie to her network. Documents, contraband, anything whatever doesn't look like it belongs on a cargo ship" I responded, shining my flashlight on a large crate with mysterious symbols.

As we ventured further into the hold, a sense of unease settled over me. The heat signature Gordo had detected was getting stronger, its source just ahead. Jack, always the strategist, signaled for us to stop. He pointed to a crate that seemed out of place—a sleek, metallic container, untouched by the sea's damage.

"There it is," Jack whispered. "That's our anomaly."

Approaching cautiously, we surrounded the crate. Payton pulled out a crowbar, opening the lid to reveal a collection of tech devices and documents. In the center was a high-tech server, its lights blinking ominously.

"Jackpot," Goose said, excitement in his eyes. "This is what we've been looking for."

"Gordo, start downloading from that server," I ordered, my mind racing with the possibilities of our discovery. "We need to know what's on there."

As Gordo got to work, I sifted through the papers and devices, my fingers brushing over evidence of Melanie's extensive operations. There were blueprints for various compounds, detailed logs of transactions, and even a few encrypted files that would require Goose's expertise to crack.

As we were each focused on our respective tasks, another discovery sent a chill down my spine. Payton, always thorough, was inspecting the cargo hold for any other secrets when he noticed something odd—a series of wires running along the floor, disappearing into the shadows. He followed them, his face growing more serious with each step.

"Boss, you might want to see this," Payton called out, his voice tinged with urgency. We gathered around him, my stomach sinking as I realized what he had found.

The wires led to a series of explosives strategically placed throughout the ship. Melanie had rigged the entire vessel to explode; she planned to destroy all evidence of her theft now that the treasure had been recovered. The timer on the detonator was counting down, a silent threat ticking away.

"Damn it, she's going to blow the ship," I hissed, my mind racing. "We need to disarm this now."

"Goose, can you handle it?" Jack asked, his voice steady despite the gravity of the situation.

"Maybe?" Goose replied, already kneeling down to examine the detonator. His fingers moved with precision, but I could see the tension in his eyes. "No. she made sure this boat was heading to the bottom. Nobody is stopping it. We've got eleven minutes to be somewhere else."

"Hurry, Gordo," I urged, my eyes flicking to the countdown. "Get that information, we don't have much time."

As Gordo worked, the rest of us kept watch, our nerves stretched thin. The minutes ticked by, each one an eternity. Finally, Gordo announced, "It's done, let's the hell outta here.

"Good work, Gordo," I said, clapping him on the shoulder. "Like you said, let's get out of here before that bomb goes off."

"Hutch, you're gonna want to see this," Gordo's voice broke through my concentration. I turned to find him holding a tablet, the drone's feed displaying a series of heat signatures moving toward the cargo hold. "We've got company... Melanie didn't evac the ship."

"She's gonna kill her own team ... Pack it up; we're moving out," I ordered, the urgency in my voice mirrored by the team's rapid movements. Payton and Jack secured the server and documents while Gordo's drone watched the approaching threats.

We retraced our steps, the tension mounting with each passing second. The exit was within sight when a sudden burst of gunfire erupted, forcing us to dive for cover. Mercenaries swarmed the hatch, their faces masked by night vision goggles and their movements precise and deadly.

"Hold them off!" I shouted, returning fire and signaling for the team to split up. Jack and Payton flanked the left, using the crates as cover, while Goose and Gordo provided suppressing fire from the right.

The firefight was intense, bullets ricocheting off the metal walls, creating a cacophony of chaos. Despite the overwhelming odds, our training and coordination gave us the upper hand. One by one, the mercenaries fell, their bodies crumpling to the floor as we advanced.

"We're clear," Jack called out, his voice strained but steady. "Let's move; we're down to less than two minutes."

We regrouped at the exit, the server downloads and documents securely in tow. The mercenaries' bodies lay scattered in our wake, a stark reminder of the peril we faced.

The cool night air greeted us as we emerged onto the deck, the stars twinkling above like distant sentinels. Our vessel waited; a beacon of safety amidst the uncertainty.

"Goose, jam their comms," I instructed, ensuring that any remaining threats would be cut off from reinforcements. "We're not taking any chances."

As Goose set to work, I turned to the team, their faces illuminated by the moon's soft glow. "We've got what we came for. Now let's get out of here."

With practiced efficiency, we scrambled back aboard our vessel, the hum of the engines a welcome sound. We had barely pulled away from the cargo ship when the explosive detonated in rapid succession, scuttling the cargo ship. I could only pray that the currents slid it left or right as it descended so it avoided the historical shipwreck, I knew lay somewhere directly below us.

Safely on our way back to shore, the adrenaline crash that always followed hit us all as the weight of our discovery settled over us. Melanie's network had been extensive, and her reach was far greater than we had anticipated. The server and documents would provide the evidence we needed to dismantle her operations piece by piece.

Once back onshore and safe, we all retreated to our respective rooms. The following morning, after a hearty breakfast, we reviewed the data, and one crucial detail emerged. Although the shipwreck had been below the cargo ship in over 400 feet of water, Melanie's operation was far ahead of what we had been led to believe. The logs and blueprints indicated that the treasure had already been recovered and moved inland to what appeared to be a series of caves near her main compound.

A compound we now knew the location of. Once she located the wreck, it appeared that she used the investment monies to fund the recovery and purchase a small cave only twelve miles from the wreck site.

I studied the blueprints more closely, realizing the true nature of the ship. It wasn't just a cargo vessel but a sophisticated recovery vehicle equipped with a moon pool at the bottom, allowing divers and submersibles to access the ocean depths directly from the ship. The moon pool was a large, open space in the hull, its edges reinforced with state-of-the-art technology designed to stabilize and protect it during underwater operations.

"This vessel served as a recovery platform," I informed the team, connecting the dots. "Melanie utilized it to salvage the treasure from the sunken ship below. They hoisted everything up through the moon pool and transported it inland to those caves."

"It's no wonder it went unnoticed. A cargo ship in these waters is as common as a fishing boat," Jack remarked, shaking his head. "I despise her, but she's devious."

"Perhaps, but we now have the proof," Goose declared, a resolute expression on his face. "We know our next move."

"Precisely," I concurred, my determination solidifying. "We must strike where it hurts and reclaim all her unlawfully acquired riches."

Chapter 14

"A man dies when he refuses to stand up for that which is right. A man dies when he refuses to stand up for justice. A man dies when he refuses to take a stand for that which is true."

— Martin Luther King Jr.

The journey back to our safe house was filled with tension but passed without any major incidents. Upon arrival, the weight of our discovery settled heavily upon us.

We dedicated the following hours to analyzing the server's data, unraveling Melanie's intricate web of deceit, and strategizing our next steps. The server contained a wealth of information, including detailed records of illegal transactions, encrypted messages with influential collaborators, and blueprints of her operations. Goose skillfully decrypted file after file, his face illuminated by the screen's glow.

"Take a look at this," Goose exclaimed, displaying a high-resolution satellite image. "Melanie's compound is located on a private island in the Exumas, a chain of over 365 islands in the Bahamas. It's a secluded and difficult-to-reach island, making it an ideal hideout."

The satellite image depicted a verdant island surrounded by the clear waters of the Caribbean. Situated within a private nature reserve, the island remained undiscovered due to its limited human activity and stringent access restrictions, providing a perfect cover for Melanie's activities. The island featured opulent villas, guarded watchtowers, and hidden entry points, with a dense jungle offering natural concealment for the compound.

"Here's the main compound," Goose continued, focusing on a cluster of buildings near the island's northern shore. "It's heavily fortified, with high walls, guard posts, and even a helipad. The place is a fortress."

Jack leaned in, examining the map closely. "Melanie's compound is fortified, but it's not impenetrable," he said, pointing to the maps and satellite images on the table. "We've faced tougher challenges."

"Here," Payton said, marking several potential entry points on the map. "These are less heavily guarded and provide natural cover. We can use the jungle to our advantage, moving stealthily until we're right on top of them."

Jack agreed, tracing possible routes with his finger. "We'll need to divide into two teams. One will create a distraction at the main entrance, diverting their attention and forces. The other will sneak in from the eastern side, utilizing the jungle cover to reach the caves where the treasure is hidden."

"We'll have to be swift and silent," I added. "The caves are accessible from within the compound, so once we're inside, we'll have to navigate through her defenses without alerting too many guards."

"I'll handle the communication blackout again," Goose mentioned, still focused on the screen. "But it won't last indefinitely. We'll need to complete our mission before they can re-establish contact with their external allies."

"Timing is crucial," Payton emphasized, pointing out the key points on the map. "We must synchronize our movements perfectly. Any delay could jeopardize the entire operation."

"Let's review the plan once more," I insisted, the determination in my voice reflected in the eyes of my team. "We cannot make any mistakes."

As the sun set behind the palm trees the following day, we approached stealthily, the ocean's gentle murmur contrasting with the pounding of my heart. Melanie's compound, a fortress of sin disguised in tropical luxury, loomed ahead. Her well-armed mercenaries patrolled the perimeter with a predator's confidence, unaware of our presence. But we were ready.

"Stay alert," I whispered over the comms, my voice steady despite the rush of adrenaline. "Focus on the objective, team."

We breached the outer fence swiftly, cutting through the metal links as if they were mere blades of grass. The silence of the evening shattered as gunfire erupted. The mercenaries were skilled, but we were better. Bullets flew past us, and I returned fire, finding comfort in the familiarity of combat.

"Move! Two o'clock!" I shouted, the sound of a grenade launcher from our side adding to the chaos. The battlefield was a symphony of violence, with gunfire and commands blending into a deadly dance.

"Payton, Jack, flank left. Advance!" I commanded, moving with determination, each step deliberate amidst the mayhem. My team trusted me, and I would not let them down. Not today.

An enemy mercenary emerged from cover, weapon raised, eyes filled with malice. Time seemed to slow as I pulled the trigger, his body falling to the ground. There was no pleasure in it, only necessity and the burden of responsibility weighing heavily on my conscience.

"Keep pushing forward!" I ordered, the leader in me taking charge, composed amid the storm of battle. "Watch each other's backs!"

We moved forward as a united group, bound by loyalty and a silent commitment to see this mission through, regardless of the sacrifices. The opulent exterior of the compound now served as the backdrop to our fierce battle, with every elegant pillar and marble statue bearing the scars of our assault.

"Initiate suppressing fire on my command!" I shouted, orchestrating our attack with the precision of a conductor. Our goal was to disrupt their formation and break their ranks. "Now!"

Bullets showered down on their positions, forcing them to take cover and allowing us to advance. We moved from one piece of cover to the next, pushing forward relentlessly, causing the mercenaries to falter. Their fear and panic only fueled our determination.

"Keep pushing! Keep pushing!" I urged, my voice cutting through the chaos. A bullet grazed my arm, but I barely felt the pain. It was a reminder of the fight we were in, a reminder that we were still alive and fighting for what was right.

"Stay focused!" I reminded them, my voice unwavering. "She's waiting for us, but she won't wait long."

As we closed in on the heart of her empire, I knew that more challenges and lives were at stake. But in that moment, standing together against the darkness she had created, I felt the unbreakable spirit of our team—a spirit forged in the face of adversity and fueled by our quest for justice. And as the final echoes of gunfire faded away, that spirit promised us victory, no matter the cost.

The massive compound towered above us, a formidable structure of concrete and steel. We were like ants in comparison, armed only with our determination and a daring plan that bordered on insanity.

Goose was bent over his makeshift console, his fingers moving swiftly across the keys with a practiced rhythm, like a conductor leading a symphony of chaos.

"Cameras are down," he whispered, a hint of satisfaction in his voice. "Melanie is blind."

I peered over Goose's shoulder, watching the lines of code scroll down the screen like a digital waterfall, obscuring the inner workings of his sabotage. The mercenaries' voices had disappeared from our earpieces, replaced by an eerie silence that spoke volumes about Goose's expertise. It It was our opportunity to capitalize on their confusion.

"Nice job, Goose." I patted him on the back, looking up at the sky where Gordo's drone hovered like a vigilant sentinel. His voice crackled over the comms, a testament to the preparation meeting opportunity.

"I've spotted two enemies flanking the east side—sending the coordinates to your HUDs."

I checked my wrist display, seeing red dots appear, revealing enemy positions with precision. Gordo's calm demeanor was contagious, calming my nerves as I relayed the information to the team.

"Adjust your approach to the east. Gordo is guiding us; let's make our path through their defenses."

We moved stealthily through the compound, with the drone providing overhead support. Gordo's updates were timely, guiding us through the chaos of battle.

"Watch your back—I see movement near the supply shed."

I turned quickly, firing at an approaching mercenary. He fell to the ground, and we continued forward, relying on Gordo's surveillance to avoid any surprises.

"The drone's battery is running low," Gordo warned urgently. "Use it wisely."

I felt the urgency in his words, knowing our tactical advantage was slipping away. We owed it to Gordo and Goose to make every decision count.

"Regroup," I ordered, scanning the path ahead. "Melanie's stronghold is within reach. Let's finish this."

As we closed in on our target, I marveled at the teamwork and skill of my friends. We moved as one, driven by a shared purpose and a thirst for justice.

Bullets flew past us as we advanced. Jack's voice cut through the chaos, guiding us through the battle.

"Delta formation," he commanded, his voice steady. We followed his lead, moving with precision and coordination.

"Suppressing fire on my signal. Three... two..." His words were the cue, and we responded with a barrage of gunfire to silence the enemy.

Payton emerged from our protective cover like a force of nature, his rifle cradled against his shoulder. There was no hesitation in his stride, only the determined drive of a man who faced fear head-on. He led the charge, weaving between cover, drawing fire, and dictating the flow of battle. His raw and unfettered laugh rang out over the gunfire—a taunt, a dare, a war cry for those who dared challenge us.

"Stay sharp," I echoed Jack's earlier command, my voice rough with adrenaline. "We move as one."

Our bullets found their targets in the chests and heads of mercenaries, their surprised faces etching into memory before they fell. Each pull of the trigger was a quest for justice—each hit a step closer to Melanie.

"Payton, left flank!" I called out, spotting the threat before it materialized. Without hesitation, Payton pivoted, taking out two foes who had tried to catch us off guard. His loyalty to the team and mission burned brightly.

"Jack, we're thin on the right!" I shouted, noting a gap in our defenses.

"Adjustment acknowledged," Jack replied calmly. "Collapse inward, maintain sight lines."

We tightened our ranks, a unified force pulsing with shared purpose. The mercenaries faltered, unable to withstand Jack's tactical skill and Payton's fearless assault. Together, we pushed forward, an unstoppable force.

"Keep the momentum," Jack urged, and we did, knowing that to slow down was to risk defeat.

With Jack's guidance and Payton's courage, we would see this through to the end.

"Down!" Goose yelled, but it was too late. Pain flared, sharp and insistent, a harsh reminder of mortality. The ground rushed up to meet me, the world narrowing to the thud of my heartbeat.

Bullets whizzed around us, a hungry swarm seeking flesh. I tracked their path, reacting instinctively as my body moved on its own. A mercenary's shot hit me, the impact knocking the breath from my lungs.

"Medic! We need a medic!" Gordo's voice cut through the haze, but I shook my head, refusing to give in.

"Leave it," I said, pressing a hand to the wound. Warm blood seeped through my fingers, a stark reminder of the danger we faced. My armor took the brunt of it.

"Stubborn as ever," Payton muttered, offering me a shoulder. Together, we rose, a symbol of resilience in the chaos.

"Goose, jam their comms!" I ordered, my vision blurring but my mind sharp.

"Already on it," Goose replied, working quickly to disrupt the mercenaries' communications. "Give me thirty seconds."

"Thirty we don't have," I countered, pushing forward despite the pain.

"Make it twenty," Jack commanded, covering Goose as he worked. The mercenaries scrambled; their radios filled with static.

"Drone's up!" Gordo announced, monitoring the compound from above. "Two enemies behind you, Hutch."

"Got it," I responded automatically, adrenaline masking the pain.

"Left side is clear," Payton reported, circling back from his charge. "We break through there."

"Move!" Jack's command spurred us into action. We moved forward with determination, crashing against Melanie's defenses like a tide against rocks.

"Jack, take point," I directed, feeling my strength waver but not my resolve. "I'll be right behind you."

"Always are," Jack retorted with a smirk in his voice amidst the chaos of battle.

"Gordo said Melanie is close," I informed the team. "There's a fortified building ahead, but it's not impenetrable."

"Nothing is," I declared, fueling our actions with belief. We moved forward, a coordinated symphony of gunfire and determination, each of us playing our part in this deadly dance.

"Clear!" The word reverberated as we breached the final room, taking down or disarming the mercenaries. Melanie's stronghold loomed ahead, a dark promise of confrontation.

"Ready?" I asked, already knowing the answer.

"Always," they replied in unison, and together, we entered the unknown, carrying the weight of the past and the focus on serving justice.

The door shattered under our combined force, revealing Melanie Lancaster, The Siren, seated like a queen amidst the chaos. She met my gaze with piercing green eyes, as if anticipating this moment.

"Melanie," I spoke calmly despite the blood loss, "it's over."

"Over?" Melanie's laughter filled the room. "You still don't understand, do you?"

I approached her, flanked by my team, a united front of determination. Gordo's equipment hummed softly, Goose's fingers flew over his tablet, cutting off her electronic escape route, and Payton's hand hovered near his sidearm, ready for action. Jack surveyed the room with unwavering focus.

"See what?" I played along with her game one last time.

"Power, Hutch. It's not about numbers or weapons," Melanie stood up slowly. "It's about control."

"You have no control now," Jack interjected, his gaze locked on hers.

"Really?" Melanie's smirk faltered. "I see five desperate men before me."

"Desperation can be a weapon too," I countered. We were weary and battered, but we stood firm.

"Perhaps," she conceded, "but so is knowledge." Her eyes flicked behind us.

"Goose?" I whispered.

"Nothing," he confirmed. There were no reinforcements coming. She had no tricks left.

"Melanie Lancaster," I declared, "you're under arrest." The weight of our struggles hung heavy in the air.

"By whose authority?" I could see in her face that Melanie's defiance was a facade, but she clung to it.

"By the lives you've destroyed," Payton's voice was resolute.

"By the justice you've eluded," Jack added.

"By the truth you've distorted," I concluded.

She stepped back, assessing the situation, still searching for an escape route. However, there was no way out. We had her cornered, each of us representing the retribution she had evaded for so long.

"Fine," she sighed, feigning surrender with grace. "Take me, then." My lawyers will have me out in an hour. This is the Bahamas.

We happily complied. The sound of handcuffs clicking was satisfying, signaling the end of the Siren's influence. "By the way you are heading to Miami, not Nassan. Some friends of ours at Homeland are looking forward to your arrival." I added enjoying the look of utter loss on Melanie's face at my words.

As we left the fortress, the weight of victory bore down on us. The compound was quiet, subdued by our attack. My wounds throbbed with each step, a reminder of the cost and the danger faced by friends. Nevertheless, we moved forward, united by more than just the mission. We had been tested by fire, our determination proven and our goal clear.

"Treasure awaits," Gordo whispered, shouldering his drone kit.

I looked at my team; their faces showed weariness but also unwavering determination. The battle of the night had taken its toll, but our task was not yet complete. The first light of dawn began to illuminate the jungle around us.

"Let's finish this," Jack said, gesturing towards the eastern side of the compound where the caves were hidden. His voice was steady, his resolve evident.

We gathered our strength and continued towards the caves, navigating the now-silent compound. Each step was intentional, each action calculated. The promise of dawn and the treasure ahead fueled our determination. The end was near, bringing justice for all of Melanie's victims.

"Ready, Hutch?" Payton inquired.

"Always," I affirmed, feeling the aches and fatigue but also the pull of adventure, urging us to close this chapter and move forward.

"Then let's go," Goose said, preparing his gadgets with anticipation in his expression.

Leaving the compound behind, we embraced the morning. The treasure awaited, hidden deep within the heart of the island. We, a group of comrades bonded through challenges, were prepared to claim it.

Our footsteps echoed the beat of justice, each stride a commitment to see it through. We had confronted danger, engaged in violence, and now, we stood on the verge of resolution. Ahead, the island held its secrets, waiting to be uncovered.

Chapter 15

"A tree that does not bend is often broken."

– Lao Tzu

Yet, the jungle still held mysteries, whispers of tales that beckoned to us. And as the sun continued its march into the sky, we stood at the entrance to a series of caves only accessible through Melanie's compound.

"Could this be it?" Catherine's voice quivered with excitement. She had joined us as we loaded Melanie and the remaining mercenaries onto a waiting police boat, that would transport them to Miami and the US Coast Guard.

"Only one way to find out." I took a step forward, the wooden stairs into the cave groaning under my weight as I descended.

We navigated through the debris, deposited by countless storms, each step leading us further into the past. Then, just past the overgrowth and debris, amidst the ruins, lay the treasure we had dared to imagine. Gold shimmered in the angled light, jewels gleamed with an inner glow, and the air buzzed with the thrill of discovery.

"Look at this ... " Gordo whispered, awe evident on his face as he lifted a gilded goblet from its murky resting place.

"Incredible," I murmured, my hands trembling as I reached for an elaborate chest. With a gentle touch, I opened the lid. The treasure inside gleamed with the promise of legends brought to life, a prize that exceeded all expectations.

"Triumph," I murmured, the word barely audible, yet it captured all we felt. After the dangerous journey, after bringing Melanie to justice, this was our prize – a tangible symbol of victory that would forever shape our lives.

Surrounded by the soft sounds of awe and quiet laughter of disbelief, I felt a sense of transition. This discovery marked the end of one journey and the start of another. The world beyond the jungle beckoned, but for now, we stood together in the midst of a revealed mystery, embracing the realization of an impossible dream.

I knelt down, gently brushing away centuries-old dried silt from a tarnished silver plate. Adorned with the crest of a forgotten lineage, it lay among the remnants of history's grandeur. Each artifact we uncovered told a story—a voyage across oceans, a legacy submerged and silenced until now.

"Be careful with that," I cautioned as Catherine carefully retrieved a rusted sextant. Her hands, steady and sure, cradled the instrument delicately. Curiosity gleamed in her eyes, mirroring the shared excitement that permeated our close-knit group. We were explorers on the cusp of rewriting history.

We meticulously cataloged each item, following the method Kate had taught us during the recovery of the Dowry of Santa Maria in Texas. Every piece was documented with the reverence befitting treasures of such significance. Bejeweled swords, fragile porcelain, coins bearing the likenesses of long-gone monarchs who once ruled vast empires—our collection expanded, a record of opulence rescued from obscurity.

"Someone will have to pry this from my cold, dead hands," Goose joked, displaying a golden cutlass with a flourish. His humor lightened the intensity of our adrenaline-fueled endeavor.

"Melanie tried, "I quipped as the final rays of sunlight filtered through the canopy above, I stepped back, seeking a moment of contemplation to fully grasp the magnitude of our find. Leaning against the weathered trunk of an ancient tree, I allowed the silence to envelop me.

The thrill of triumph still coursed through me, but as the initial excitement ebbed, introspection took hold. This treasure, vast and incomprehensible, held the power to alter everything. For years, I had navigated life's uncertainties, searching for purpose beyond the horizon. Now, with this treasure within reach, the path ahead shimmered with newfound clarity.

The wealth could bring transformation, not just for me, but for countless others—if handled with care. The weight of responsibility loomed large. I thought of the small farming community that shaped me, the hands that guided me in my youth. They deserved more than tales of adventure; they deserved to share in the rewards of it.

"Are you thinking about home?" Catherine's voice interrupted my thoughts.

"Always," I responded, my eyes fixed on the horizon. "But I'm thinking on a larger scale now."

"Good. Because this is just the beginning, Hutch." She pointed to the treasure, her smile a challenge and a promise.

"Indeed, it is," I agreed, feeling a sense of determination growing within me. Whatever lay ahead, my path was guided by ambition and a moral compass ingrained in my soul.

As night fell, I stood up, ready to rejoin the group. We had faced danger, delivered justice, and uncovered marvels. Tomorrow would mark the start of a new chapter, but for now, we celebrated the culmination of our relentless pursuit.

"Let's secure these artifacts," I called out confidently. "There's much work to be done."

And so, under the cover of twilight, we labored to protect remnants of a bygone era for a future yet to be written.

I uncorked a bottle of twenty-year-old Texas bourbon, the aged cork popping satisfyingly. The amber liquid poured into makeshift cups, our treasure trove offering more than just riches and relics but also moments of joy.

"Here's to us," I toasted, raising my cup beneath the starlit sky above our island camp.

"Here's to us!" the group echoed in unison, their faces illuminated by the campfire's glow and our triumph. Goose's laughter mingled with Jeremy's deeper chuckle as they clinked cups, the sound as rich as the treasures beneath our feet.

We drank deeply, the bourbon's warmth a comforting contrast to the night's chill. For a brief moment, the world outside our circle faded away, leaving only the bond of comradeship forged through challenges and victories.

"Never thought we'd see something like this," Goose admitted, his eyes gleaming in the firelight. "But here we are."

"Perhaps it's divine providence?" Jeremy suggested, a hint of mischief in his eyes.

"Or just damn good luck," I countered, my grin matching the vast expanse before us.

Jeremy nodded thoughtfully. "The Good Book says it's easier for a camel to pass through the eye of a needle than for a rich man to enter the kingdom of God. But it's what we do with our wealth that truly matters."

"Here's to a brighter future," Jeremy proclaimed, raising his cup once more.

"Here's to a brighter future," we repeated, our voices blending together in a pledge carried on the winds of change.

In that shared vow, I found the true treasure. Not the glittering coins or priceless artifacts, but the connection between us and the collective determination to shape a better world.

I dialed a number on the satellite phone, reaching out to a contact reserved for moments of utmost discretion and trust. The full moon had risen, casting long shadows on the sand like fingers reaching out to claim the treasures we had discovered.

"Dr. Kate Bannister," I said as the call connected, my voice steady despite the lingering excitement. She was a renowned expert in maritime archaeology, known for her successful preservations.

"Kate, it's Hutch Holub. We have a delicate situation here—a promising one, but delicate." I could almost sense her curiosity piqued on the other end of the line.

"Tell me more, Hutch."

"Are you familiar with The Isabella, a Spanish ship lost in 1757?" I asked, knowing it was one of her passions since college.

"Don't play games with me, Hutch. I know you too well. What's going on?" she inquired.

"We've found her... and her cargo. Unfortunately, the ship was mostly destroyed, but the cargo was preserved. We need your expertise, Kate. We want to handle this by the book—preserved, cataloged, the whole nine yards," I explained.

A sharp intake of breath indicated her understanding of the gravity of the discovery. "You really found the Isabella, Hutch? My God, after all these years of searching. I'll get the team ready. Coordinates?"

"Actually, Melanie Lancaster found her…and looted her." I explained, recounting how we had discovered the ship just after Melanie had stripped it clean and then tracked Melanie and the cargo back to the cave. I proceeded to provide all the relevant information while observing Goose and Jeremy meticulously cataloging the smaller artifacts. They handled history with reverence, knowing that each piece was part of a larger narrative spanning centuries.

"Wait, the Bahamas is very strict regarding archaeological finds…Authorities?" she inquired, referring to the locals.

"Already briefed and on board. We were fortunate to come across someone who was helpful in our search and also acted as a liaison with the local authorities. You'll meet Catherine when you arrive at the site. She ensured that they understood the significance—and the necessity for discretion."

"Good. Expect us within forty-eight…make it twenty-four, hours. You really found her?" Kate pondered.

"Appreciated, Kate. See you then."

The call concluded, and a sense of professionalism enveloped me like a cloak. It wasn't just about discovering treasure—it was about preserving the past for the future. A future in which I suddenly had a strong interest.

"Is everything in order?" Catherine's voice came softly from behind me, her presence a comforting warmth in the evening chill.

"Everything is set," I replied, turning to face her. The moon light cast a gentle glow on her features, softening the lines of concentration that had marked her face during our quest.

"Good. Because I've been thinking…" She hesitated, a rare occurrence since I had met her.

"About?" I inquired, moving closer.

"Us, Hutch. What comes next. After the dust settles and the credits roll."

A smile played at the corner of my mouth. "I believe life is more than a movie, darlin. But if you're asking if I see you in my future, the answer is as clear as the ocean before us."

Her eyes met mine, searching, finding truth in the depths of blue. "I want to build something with you, Hutch. Something genuine. Not just chasing thrills or evading ghosts like I was when I first came to these islands."

"Then let's build," I said, taking her hands in mine. "Let's seize this opportunity to create a world where thrills come from creation, not destruction. Where the only ghosts are the ones we put to rest with every good deed we perform."

"Sounds like a plan," she whispered, her smile reflecting mine.

We lingered there for a moment longer, two souls anchored amidst the tide of change, before turning back to rejoin the others. Our unspoken pact was as solid as the earth beneath our feet, a silent agreement to face whatever lay ahead together.

A bright moon hung high, casting elongated shadows across the white sands as I gathered our diverse group in a loose circle. Jeremy stood firm, with his hands clasped behind him like a general addressing his troops. Goose's playful smirk had transformed into a look of contemplation, his eyes fixed on the horizon. Catherine leaned casually against a palm tree, her gaze steady and confident.

"Friends," I began, my voice carrying over the gentle waves, "we have weathered storms together, both literal and metaphorical."

Goose interjected, "And dodged more bullets than I can count on my fingers and toes."

A round of chuckles lightened the mood, but the seriousness of our situation brought us back to the present. I locked eyes with each of them in turn. "Like when we found the Santa Maria we have a choice. We can part ways, enriched by our experiences, or we can use what we have discovered here to continue building something enduring. A legacy that transcends mere riches and artifacts. The Horizon' Foundation "

Catherine stepped forward, the ocean breeze tousling her hair. "This treasure is meaningless without a purpose. It is what we do with it that gives it significance. We can use it to preserve history, change lives, and champion causes worth fighting for."

As the moon disappeared into the clouds and darkness fell, we packed up our things and left the island. It was peaceful, with only the sound of the tide and the rustling leaves. We headed to the boat for the night, guards stationed at the caves. Each step felt significant, as we embraced our new mission. I looked back, taking in the place where we had become allies, now united by a common fate.

"Ready to get some sleep?" Catherine asked, holding my hand.

"Sleep? Eventually," I replied with a smile.

Chapter 16

"To strive tirelessly and at all times to reach one's goal — therein lies the secret of success."

— Anna Pavlova

The cerulean waves welcomed us back, their rhythmic lapping against the hull a comforting sound after the challenging weeks we had faced. Kate had responded promptly to my call, and upon her arrival, she immediately began the process of recovery. She brought in a second team to handle the recovery and cataloging of the ship, which had been stripped by Melanie for its cargo. Fortunately, the captain's quarters remained mostly untouched, allowing us to salvage much of its contents.

As our ship, now laden with treasure chests and the weight of our adventures, approached the familiar docks of Nassau, I stood at the bow with my cowboy hat shielding my eyes from the Bahamian sun, feeling the salt on my skin. We had achieved our goal - reclaiming what was taken and settling old scores. The elation of victory was mixed with a profound sense of relief.

"Land ho, Hutch," Goose's voice rang out, filled with satisfaction as he expertly navigated the rigging.

"It's good to be back, isn't it?" Jeremy's deep voice resonated from behind me as he stood like a watchful guardian, scanning the horizon with his gray eyes.

"It sure is," I replied, tipping my hat back to meet his gaze. "We delivered justice to those who believed they were untouchable."

Kate joined us at the railing, her hair fluttering in the breeze. "And you did it together," she remarked, her hazel eyes hinting at untold tales.

As we approached the dock, Catherine's figure became more distinct, standing out from the busy crowd. She had been my guiding light throughout this journey, a source of strength during the toughest times.

"It's time to bid farewell, everyone," I announced, the words feeling solemn as they left my lips.

We disembarked, each of us carrying a part of the history we had uncovered. The sound of gold clinking accompanied our steps as I made my way to Catherine. She greeted me with a smile, a mixture of pride and sadness evident in her expression.

"I never expected to find a family on a treasure hunt," she remarked, her voice steady yet filled with emotion.

"Neither did I," I replied, embracing Catherine warmly.

We had returned with more than just riches; we carried stories of daring escapes and hard-fought battles that had tested our resolve to the limit.

"It's hard to believe it's all come to an end," Goose commented, joining me by the railing. His gaze was contemplative, lost in thought.

"Every bruise, every near miss... they were all worth it," Jeremy added, his deep voice blending with the gentle sound of the water.

Kate stood next to him, her eyes shining with the light of the setting sun. "We've emerged from this experience stronger, more knowledgeable," she reflected. "Not many can claim to have faced danger head-on and emerged richer in more ways than one."

I nodded, the significance of their words sinking in as deeply as the anchor we would soon drop upon reaching the harbor. "We've been through a lot together, but we did it as a team. The unity we found, the justice we brought to all those Melanie had wronged, that's the true treasure."

Chapter 17

"The sun at home warms better than the sun elsewhere."

— Albanian Proverb

The plane's wheels touched down, marking the end of our latest adventure. Looking out the window, I saw the familiar Texas landscape unfolding below. The tarmac stretched out, a grey ribbon against the green backdrop. A sense of relief washed over me as the engines quieted down.

"Welcome home, Hutch," Goose said softly from the seat beside me.

"It does feel good," I replied, adjusting my hat. "Who would've thought a fishing tournament and vacation would turn into four months away?"

Stepping off the plane, the warm Texas wind enveloped me like a hug. Brother Jeremy led the way, his shoulders finally relaxed. As we entered the terminal, our people greeted us with tears and smiles that outshone the sun.

"Tinker!" I heard the familiar voice and found myself in my father's embrace. His presence grounded me like nothing else could. Tinker, his nickname for me, brought back memories of childhood mischief.

Amidst the laughter and joy of reunion, we found a moment of quiet reflection back at the ranch house. The celebration continued around us, but we were content in our own little world.

"We did well out there," Jeremy's voice rumbled, his gaze distant but content.

"More than well," I added, swirling the amber liquid in my glass. "We faced down threats that would've broken lesser men."

"Threats we'll likely be facing again, knowing this crew," Goose quipped, leaning back in his chair, the light catching the mischief still living in his eyes. "But like every adventure we've been on, military or not, we're not the same men who left this place. We're stronger now."

"Sharper," I agreed. "And armed with lessons that only the kind of danger we've danced with can teach."

"Justice has its price," Jeremy intoned, his gray eyes locking onto mine. "We paid some of it, but there's always more due."

"Consequences," I echoed, feeling the truth of his words deep in my bones. "Yes, there will always be consequences … but that also means older and wiser."

"Wouldn't have it any other way," Goose concluded, raising his glass. "To justice and the bonds that don't break."

"To justice … not to mention older and wiser," Jeremy and I echoed with a grin, our glasses meeting in the space between us, a silent vow for the future.

In the reflection of the glass, I saw not only my own weathered face but also the faces of my brothers-in-arms, my family. I knew that whatever challenges lay ahead, we would face them together because that is who we are and what we do. Thumbing the edge of the old map, its corners worn from weeks in my jacket pocket, I knew the wealth it led us to could make a significant impact on many lives. It was securely held in a trust, awaiting our next move.

"Expanding the Horizons Foundation," I began, breaking the silence that enveloped our small group. "That's our first step."

Jeremy nodded, his fingers tapping a rhythm on the oak table. "Maybe we could create a program for education, especially for kids who have faced adversity like we did." Goose added, his eyes shining with determination, "And we need to make a real difference, not just throw money at the problem. We need to be actively involved."

"Agreed," I said firmly, the decision settling within me. This treasure, akin to the Dowry of Santa Maria, was hard-earned and would not be wasted on trivial pursuits. We would use it to revitalize neglected and exploited areas, bringing new life to the world.

"Okay." I rose from my seat, feeling the weight of responsibility settling on my shoulders—a burden I knew well. "I'll contact the executive director of the foundation tomorrow to kick things off, and then we can all meet as a team to iron out the details."

"Just make sure they understand it's not just about money … it's about empowerment, impact, and leaving a lasting legacy," Jeremy emphasized, his eyes meeting mine.

"Got it." I adjusted my hat, contemplating the task ahead. Ensuring the proper management and distribution of the treasure was crucial. It wasn't just wealth; it was a tool, a way to bring a bit of justice to an unjust world.

"Here's to us," I toasted, raising my glass. The liquid shimmered in the light, a reminder of the wealth we had discovered.

We all took a sip, the sharp taste of the alcohol grounding us in reality amidst our lofty aspirations. For a moment, the outside world faded away, leaving just us—the triumphant ones, the protectors of fortune, bound by more than just the thrill of the hunt.

As the night grew darker, with its familiar sights and sounds, our Bahamian escapade gently slipped into the past. But the future lay ahead, unwritten, beckoning us to embark on our next great journey.

The world awaited our exploration, our impact. Together.

Epilogue

"Faith is taking the first step, even when you don't see the whole staircase."

– Martin Luther King Jr.

It had been nearly half a year since our return to Texas, and I sat in a conference room where the screen displayed "The Golden Rule in Leadership: Aligning Purpose for Success" by Dr. Ty H. Wenglar, PhD. Each word on the screen felt like a steppingstone toward the man I aspired to be—for my team, for Catherine. Adjusting the brim of my cowboy hat, a gesture as familiar as breathing, I leaned in, absorbing the wisdom being shared. The speaker, a former military man with a commanding voice, delved into leadership in the civilian world. His words resonated with my own experiences but offered new perspectives on navigating the chaos we often encountered.

"Make decisions decisively, take action promptly, and above all, consider all stakeholders, not just shareholders," he proclaimed, and a realization dawned on me. Leadership wasn't merely about issuing commands; it was about bearing the responsibility of those decisions, guiding a team through turbulent times. As he shared anecdotes, I jotted down notes, not just to remember but to internalize to integrate these teachings into the core of who I was.

Meanwhile, Catherine was holed up in her study, typing away furiously as she turned our adventures into a story. I pictured her deep in concentration, a little wrinkle forming above her nose that I found endearing, her fingers flying across the keyboard with the same precision she used in navigating ruins or disarming traps. Through her writing, she aimed to immortalize our journey, sharing our successes and struggles with a world unaware of the dangers we encountered. Her determination to tell our tale inspired me, much like my father did.

I had been making the rounds, checking in on each team member over the past few days. With all the media attention on the discovery and Melanie's arrest, I wanted to make sure everyone was doing okay.

Goose's workspace was a stark contrast to Catherine's study, filled with gadgets and tools, his mind as quick as his hands. He was focused on developing technology that could help us in our future missions—a drone for mapping unexplored areas, or a device to counter poachers' weapons. His humor was a shield, but underneath it was a strong determination to protect the vulnerable.

A few blocks away, Gordo was surrounded by eager young tech enthusiasts, each eager to learn from his expertise. He emphasized the beauty of simplicity, guiding them through circuit boards and code with patience. His mentorship was invaluable to these budding technologists, their skills blossoming under his guidance like plants reaching for sunlight.

Gordo's commitment was a silent reflection of his character—a man who recognized that true strength came from empowering others. As the young minds around him began to grasp the concepts he effortlessly wielded, I felt a swell of pride. We were more than adventurers; we were mentors, creators, innovators—shapers of our destiny and the world's.

Though our individual pursuits may have seemed different, they were connected by a shared desire to surpass our past selves. We looked inward to reach outward, understanding that growth was not just a personal achievement but the foundation of our unity. Each step we took alone strengthened the steps we would take together, facing whatever challenges lay ahead.

After completing the usual ranch tasks in the morning and with the sun now high in the sky, I discovered Payton knee-deep in the debris of a storm-damaged home. He handled a hammer with precision, his actions purposeful. This community project was his latest endeavor—a tangible expression of his determination to rebuild what adversity had destroyed.

"Hutch," he called out, noticing me amidst the rubble, a smile breaking through the dust on his face. "Grab a tool and lend a hand. There's healing in helping."

I took a shovel, feeling the cold, solid metal in my grip. Together, we worked in silence, allowing our labor to speak for us. Payton's enthusiasm was contagious, his resolve unwavering in the face of widespread destruction. He was not just rebuilding walls; he was restoring spirits, including his own.

Every nail hammered, every board placed, was a small triumph against the forces that sought to extinguish hope. Payton understood that adventure was not always about the thrill of the unknown; sometimes, it was about the bravery to repair what was familiar and cherished. His selflessness was as integral to him as his adventurous nature—a silent promise to leave the world in a better state than he found it.

During each of my visits, I had invited the team to the ranch for steaks and beers. In truth, it was simply a good excuse to gather the team, my family, together. That night, after a meal of our customary grilled steaks and perhaps one too many Lone Star Beers, we found ourselves beneath a canopy of stars, sharing laughter and aspirations until the embers of our fire glowed softly, offering warmth in the cool night.

In the ensuing quiet, I pondered the uncertain paths ahead. Yet, with these steadfast companions by my side, I knew we could confront whatever challenges awaited us beyond the horizon. Together, we were a formidable force, a testament to the enduring strength of unity in the wilderness of this uncharted world.

Later that night, after the team had left or crashed in the bunkhouse, I sat at my old mahogany desk, idly tracing the scars etched into the wood—each a testament to battles fought and lessons learned. The wind whispered through the open window, carrying the scent of mesquite and a hint of adventures beyond the ranch's horizon. The quiet allowed for reflection, and I let my mind wander down the winding path of my leadership journey.

The weight of responsibility had always been a familiar companion, a constant reminder that others looked to me for guidance. In the room's silence, I acknowledged the pride I felt, not from accolades or victories, but from witnessing the growth of those I'd led. From Hutchins Holub, the boy who herded cattle with his grandaddy and farmed Rice with his father under the vast Texas sky, to Hutch, the man ready to shepherd his team through life's tempests—I had come far.

"Lost in thought?" Catherine's voice cut through the stillness, as soothing as a gentle river's melody.

I glanced up, meeting her gaze. "Just charting the course ahead," I replied, my voice steady.

She pulled a chair beside me, her presence grounding me in my introspection. "You're the leader you were meant to be, Hutch."

"Have I?" Doubt flickered in my thoughts.

"Absolutely." Her conviction was reassuring. "And yet, there's more to you than just the leader, the protector. There's the man I love—the one building a future with me."

Her words comforted me, easing the weariness that sometimes-crept in. "We're both more than the sum of our parts, darlin'."

"Reckon so," she teased, mimicking my Texas twang. "Our future's wide open, Hutch. Where do you see us heading?"

"Wherever the road takes us, as long as it's together." My response was unwavering. "We've got ambitions as big as the sky, Catherine. You with your writing, me with … well, whatever comes next."

"Whatever comes next," she echoed softly, leaning into me. "Together."

"Always." The word hung between us, a promise.

We sat next to each other, connected by dreams and determination. Outside, the landscape extended endlessly, a reminder of the uncharted territory of life. But inside, within our shared vision, I felt a sense of wholeness that surpassed any adventure.

In that moment, the uncertainties of the future didn't seem as intimidating. With Catherine beside me, I felt the beginnings of a new journey, one defined not by danger or violence, but by the pursuit of happiness and the creation of a legacy based on justice and consequence.

As the night grew darker, the stars witnessed our plans, our love, and the unwritten chapters of our lives waiting for the first light of day. Together, we would confront the unknown, united by a love as vast as the Texas sky and as enduring as the principles that had shaped us.

"When are you starting the church renovation in San Antonio for Horizons? Are you excited to return to your construction roots?" Catherine asked, her voice filled with anticipation.

"Ready as I'll ever be," I replied, and I meant it.

Made in the USA
Columbia, SC
14 October 2024